CODENAME **QUICKSILVER**

Adrenaline Rush

Look out for the other
CODENAME **QUICKSILVER** books

In the Zone

The Tyrant King

Burning Sky

KillChase

End Game

CODENAME
QUICKSILVER

Adrenaline
Rush

Allan Jones

Orion
Children's Books

With special thanks to Rob Rudderham.

First published in Great Britain in 2013
by Orion Children's Books
a division of the Orion Publishing Group Ltd
Orion House
5 Upper St Martin's Lane
London WC2H 9EA
An Hachette UK company

1 3 5 7 9 10 8 6 4 2

The Orion Publishing Group's policy is to use papers that are natural, renewable and recyclable products and made from wood grown in sustainable forests. The logging and manufacturing processes are expected to conform to the environmental regulations of the country of origin. A catalogue record for this book is available from the British Library.

ISBN 978 1 4440 0549 3

Printed in Great Britain by Clays Ltd, St Ives plc

For Rod, a great friend and constant inspiration

CHAPTER **ONE**

HOLLYWOOD, CALIFORNIA.
FORTY-FIFTH DAY OF SHOOTING THE
MOVIE *ADRENALINE RUSH.*
LOCATION OF SHOOT: BENEDICT CANYON.

"Action!"

Zak was jogging on the spot, loosening his limbs, getting his body ready. At the sound of the director's voice, he snapped into focus and raced forwards. He ignored the camera operators and the swinging boom mikes and all the other people out of shot. He concentrated on the point where a narrow side street opened out to the long slope of the main road.

The bus would appear any moment now.

He could hear it coming – engine gunning, wheels on tarmac.

He was almost at his mark – the chalk line on the road that meant he was in view of the cameras.

The yellow school bus came barrelling down the hill, passing the end of the side street in a flash. Zak grinned, loving this. He leaned into his run, putting on a spurt of speed that took him into shot.

The bus was packed with seven-year-old kids. Zak could hear them yelling their heads off just like the director had told them to. "You're really scared, okay? The bus driver has had a heart attack. The bus is running out of control. Plenty of yelling and screaming, guys."

Zak hared out onto the main road, swerving to follow the careering bus. He saw panicky faces at the windows, fists beating on the glass, mouths stretched wide. The kids were really getting into it.

He'd been told to make it look good. Not too easy. To make it seem as if the bus was getting away from him. Don't worry about facial expressions – if we get a good shot of your face, we'll strip it out for the real actor in post-production.

Zak was just the stand-in, the stunt person. Because Zak could do the running for real. And that was what this action movie was all about – reality!

He slowed a little, letting the bus gain a lead on him. The director wanted effort and drama, and Zak was prepared to give it to him. After all, it wasn't every day he got asked to appear in a Hollywood blockbuster.

The voice of Grayson Clarke, the director, sang out in his earpiece. "That's great, Zak – now go for it."

"On it!" Zak moved up a gear, chasing the bus for real now, seeing the kids' faces staring out of the back window as he drew closer. Then he caught up and ran alongside the bus, spotting the cameras following the action out of the corner of his eye.

The door opposite the driver's seat was open. He gave a final burst of speed.

This was the tricky bit. He had to reach for the rail and pull himself on board. He'd been practising for the last two days with some of the professional stunt men. If he got it wrong and fell on his face, not only would he feel like a total idiot, but they'd have to start the scene from scratch. The producer, Elton Dean, wouldn't be happy. He was constantly marching around the set telling everyone that time was money.

Concentrate! Zak told himself. *Get it right.*

Zak snatched hold of the rail and boosted himself up onto the lowest step of the bus.

Perfect.

"That's excellent, Zak!" Grayson Clarke's voice was in his ear again. "Keep up the energy level. You're doing fine work."

"No problem," Zak said, speaking into the tiny mike that was attached to the lapel of his leather jacket.

The stunt driver – a really nice guy called Chet – was slumped over the wheel of the bus just as he'd been instructed.

Heart attack. Foot jammed down on the gas pedal. Bus out of control. Arrgh! Who will save the day?

Zak flung himself onto the steps, his ears now filled with the screaming of the kids. He had to admire their energy. Somewhere among them was Elton Dean's own nephew, Brandon Fine. Zak had met him briefly – a mouthy little kid with plenty of attitude.

Zak found his balance on the speeding bus then approached the driver. *Shake him by the shoulders. Yell in his ear.* "Are you okay, mister?" His voice wasn't being recorded, so it didn't really matter, but the director said it would help him "keep in the moment" if he followed the script.

Chet was a real pro. He showed no signs of life as Zak grabbed him and hauled him out of the seat. There was blood on the front of Chet's shirt. That was weird. Zak hadn't been told there'd be blood.

"Keep the action moving, Zak," came Grayson Clarke's voice in his ear.

"I'm on it." Zak assumed they'd explain about the blood later. He dragged Chet from the seat and let him slump on the floor between the driver's station and the steps. Then Zak jumped into the seat, grabbed the big steering wheel in both hands and stamped down hard on the brakes.

Oh, yes! This was the movies!

The bus didn't slow. Zak stared between his knees. The brake was marked with a big X so he couldn't get it wrong. He stamped again on the pedal marked X.

The bus just kept on going. In fact, it was speeding up now as the hill became steeper.

"Zak, you can stop the bus now," Grayson Clarke instructed.

"I'm trying to," Zak replied. He put his foot down again on the brake. It felt strangely loose, as if it wasn't connected to anything.

"Zak, you've passed your mark – stop the bus!" the director shouted.

"It's not working!" This wasn't in the script. What was he supposed to do?

Zak could hear Grayson Clarke. He was speaking to someone else now, but not bothering to cover the mike. "Amateurs!" he growled. "We should never have used amateurs." Zak started to feel worried. The director thought this was his fault.

Zak nudged Chet with his foot. "Chet, something's gone wrong," he shouted above the racket the kids were kicking up. "The brake isn't working! Chet! I can't stop the bus. *Chet!*"

He gave the stuntman a hard kick. The slumped body rolled onto its side on the floor of the bus. Zak saw that the patch of blood on Chet's shirtfront was larger now. And there was more blood on the floor.

He was beginning to get a bad feeling about this. But then, this was the movies – you couldn't believe anything you saw in the movies. It was all special effects . . . wasn't it?

"Hey, you chump, stop the bus!" Zak glanced over his shoulder at the sound of the angry voice. It was Brandon Fine. He was standing up and glaring at Zak from the middle of the bus. Zak didn't much like Brandon – he was seven going on thirty-five and ever since he'd turned up on location he'd been talking as if he was running the entire shoot. That's what comes of being the nephew of a Hollywood movie producer, Zak guessed.

"How dumb *are* you?" Brandon demanded. "You missed the mark, genius!" The other kids had stopped acting as well. They were staring at him, confused now.

"Calm down," Zak called to them. "Everything's fine."

"What a loser!" Brandon said, rolling his eyes.

Zak had more important things to do than argue with a stroppy seven year old.

Keeping one hand on the steering wheel, he leaned over and felt for the carotid artery on Chet's neck.

Nothing. No pulse. Chet was dead.

Zak's heart punched against his ribs. This was real.

He didn't want to panic the kids. They mustn't know what had happened. The footbrake had failed, but he wasn't out of options yet. He snatched hold of the handbrake and yanked at it. It moved easily in his hand, connected to nothing. Useless. What was going on here?

He had one last idea. He twisted the keys in the ignition and pulled them out.

The engine kept going, the bus hurtled onwards. He could hear Grayson Clarke's voice yelling in his ear, "Get Chet to stop the bus!"

He ignored the director. He couldn't think of anything to say that wouldn't freak the kids out.

Grayson Clarke was still yelling. "What are you waiting for?"

Will you shut up; I'm trying to think.

Zak gripped the steering wheel, his knuckles white. He was on his own with this – he had to come up with a way of stopping the bus. It wasn't easy with the road whipping away under the wheels and the hill getting steeper by the second. Some of the kids had started whimpering.

"Everything's fine!" Zak shouted back to them. "Just stay in your seats and hold tight."

He dropped his chin, trying to get his mouth as close to the mike as possible.

"The brakes aren't working," he said, hoping the kids wouldn't be able to hear him. "Chet can't help." Zak's voice died in his throat. He had just spotted something that set his heart pounding.

There was a small neat hole high in the windscreen, close to the driver's rear-view mirror. A hole no bigger than his little finger, with a spiderweb of cracks around it.

A bullet hole.

Chet had been shot dead and the bus had been sabotaged. For some reason someone wanted to put these kids in real danger. Zak clamped his fingers around the wheel, staring ahead, trying to come up with a plan.

The long hill descended for about another 500 metres before it levelled out and met the main four-lane highway. Zak could see the cars and trucks streaming past in both directions. If he couldn't stop the bus, it would smash right into the traffic.

Zak didn't have time to be stunned or scared or freaked out. He had to do something. And quickly.

The long hill began to curve a little and Zak saw there was a solid stone wall running down one side. The shred of a plan came into his mind. Grayson Clarke was still shouting in his ear, but he couldn't let himself be distracted. He ripped out the earpiece. Behind him, some of the kids were crying and sobbing – they'd figured out that something had gone wrong. Even Brandon had gone quiet.

Ignore them. Concentrate.

Zak turned the steering wheel, driving the bus towards the edge of the road. He gritted his teeth, hoping he wasn't about to get them all killed. The wall loomed closer. He eased the wheel around a fraction more.

The bus shuddered and shook as the front bumper made contact with the wall. The wheel juddered in Zak's hands. There was a screaming noise as metal grazed against stone.

Carefully. Not too hard. Gritting his teeth, Zak kept the wheel locked, holding the bus against the wall. The grinding and screeching noise filled the bus.

"Get on the floor! Cover your faces!" Zak yelled. Kids flung themselves out of their seats, falling in heaps into the aisle and between the seats.

The sound of metal on stone was mind-shredding. Zak's whole body shook. He saw sparks and shards of stone flying into the air. The side of the bus was being ripped apart.

But it seemed to be working. The friction was beginning to slow the bus down.

The jolting in his arms was almost too painful to bear, but he refused to give in. Using every ounce of strength, he leaned against the wheel. Pieces of stone smashed through the windows, ricocheting all around. Showers of sparks spewed upwards. There was a horrible burning smell – hot metal and smouldering rubber.

Still Zak struggled with the wheel. The highway was only a hundred metres away now, filled with racing traffic.

A block of stonework jutted out from the wall. Zak just had time to see that it was one side of a gateway before the bus struck it. The windscreen disintegrated and chunks of stone cascaded into the bus. He ducked, feeling them hitting him and bouncing off. The impact caused the nearside of the bus to buckle, punching sharp-edged pieces of metal perilously close to Zak's legs.

The bus slewed around and tipped dangerously. For a moment Zak was afraid the whole thing would topple onto its side. Then it righted itself, crashed down on its wheels and came to a screeching halt.

Gasping with relief, Zak collapsed over the steering wheel.

He felt as though every bone in his body had been jarred loose. He felt like throwing up. His body ached.

But he had done it.

The sound of kids screaming roused him. He sat up and looked over his shoulder. Flames were licking around the outside of the bus. The friction must have set something on fire.

He staggered to his feet. "Come on," he yelled over the screaming. "We have to get out of here." Zak reached down and pulled Chet's limp body to one side. The kids began to tumble forwards, barging and jostling as they fought to get through the doors. They looked utterly terrified as Zak guided them off the bus.

The flames were rising now, advancing through the broken windows. The bus was filling with smoke. Zak coughed, blinking, his eyes stinging. He caught the last kid by the shoulder. A blonde girl with a ponytail and huge frightened blue eyes.

"Is there anyone else back there?" he asked her.

She stared at him for a moment then ripped herself free and dived down the steps.

Zak peered into the billowing smoke.

"Anyone there?" he shouted. He could hardly see, and his ears were still ringing from the noise of the crash. "*Anyone*?"

He crouched, trying to get down where the smoke was less thick. He could see a few bags and coats strewn across the floor. He saw a bundle about halfway down. Jammed between the seats. A coat?

"Hey!"

Was that a voice he could hear back there? The crackling of the flames made it hard to be sure.

He had done a firefighting course in training. He tried to remember what he'd been taught. Keep low in a smoke-filled room was one lesson he remembered very well. He flattened himself on his belly and edged forwards.

Coughing, and with streaming eyes, Zak headed for the bundle. The flames were leaping yellow and red through the pall of smoke. He could feel the heat on his face, scorching his clothes. Grimacing, he moved closer and reached under the seat.

There was a hand. He opened his mouth to say something reassuring, but found he couldn't speak. His breath was coming in choking gasps and he was almost blinded. He closed his fingers around the wrist and pulled, dragging the child along with him.

He was close to the exit now. The metal ridge of the top step was under his feet. He got to his knees, retching and unable to see much more than a dark blur. He could hear the boy coughing. He must have been knocked unconscious – but he was coming around.

Zak grabbed the limp bundle under the arms and stumbled down the steps, falling, turning so the kid didn't hit the tarmac first.

He could hear people yelling. Feet running. Someone took the kid from his arms. Someone else picked Zak up and carried him away from the bus.

"I'm okay," he panted. "Let me down."

He was put onto his feet.

"Chet is still in there," someone else shouted. "We have to get him out."

Zak swayed, his lungs hurting, his vision blurred. He rubbed the smoky tears out of his eyes.

"He's dead," he gasped.

"Are you sure?"

"He was shot," said Zak.

"He was *what*?"

Zak's head was swimming. "Someone shot him through the windscreen," he gasped. "And someone wrecked the brakes." He wiped his grimy sleeve across his face. "This wasn't an accident – this was deliberate."

A babble of voices surrounded him.

"What did the kid say?"

"That's crazy!"

"Forget it – no way was anyone shot!"

Zak didn't argue. He'd be proved right when the police arrived and did their forensics.

He stared across the road. The back end of the bus was full of leaping flames. Ugly black smoke billowed up. The kids were on the other side of the road, huddled together, crying, terrified, being comforted by adults.

Someone ran towards the bus. "We have to get Chet!"

"He's dead!" Zak yelled. But the man ignored him.

A voice called out urgently. "Keep back – the gas tank could blow!"

The man hesitated, already halfway across the road. He was still standing there when a fierce explosion rocked the bus and a plume of oily black and red fire rolled up into the sky. The man turned and ran, his arms up to cover his head. A couple of metres closer and he'd have gone up with the bus.

Zak reeled back from the searing heat.

If he hadn't stayed and checked, the kid would be dead. He wiped his sleeve over his dirty, sweating face. The boy he'd saved was standing close by, conscious now and shaking. It was Brandon Fine.

CHAPTER **TWO**

TWO HOURS LATER.

"Hey, Silver, I've got Colonel Hunter and Assistant Director Reed on conference-vid," called Wildcat.

Zak was in the small bathroom of a movie trailer, drying himself after a much-needed shower. "Coming," he called, flinging on some clean clothes.

The trailer was one of a dozen or more standing in a car park a few hundred metres away from where they had been filming. It was a good place for Zak and Wildcat to hang out between shots. One thing Zak had quickly realized was that movie-making involved a whole lot of waiting around while shots were being set up.

The two Project 17 agents were in California at the request of FBI Assistant Director Isadora Reed. She had been in London a while back, and she'd visited Fortress, the underground base where the specialist department of British Intelligence known as Project 17 had its headquarters. She'd seen Zak Archer – codename Quicksilver – in action. She'd been impressed.

Project 17 was an unusual set-up. Its agents were all in their teens; highly trained, highly motivated young people who could be sent at a moment's notice into extreme danger in any part of the world. Their unique ability was to blend in and to go unnoticed in situations where adult agents might arouse an enemy's suspicions.

At first, Colonel Hunter, Project 17's Commander, had been reluctant to lend such uniquely talented agents to the FBI. Terrorist threats were growing in Europe and the UK – there was plenty of vital work to be done on their side of the Atlantic. Zak wasn't in on the video-link negotiations that had gone on between AD Reed and Colonel Hunter behind closed doors – all he knew was what the Colonel told him afterwards.

He could still remember almost every word the Colonel had said.

"The FBI have asked me if I would be prepared to loan you to them for a very special mission, Quicksilver. They have asked for you especially because of your abilities." That meant they needed someone quick on their toes. Zak had a freaky adrenaline imbalance that allowed him to run super-fast. *"I've agreed that you will be seconded to the FBI for the duration of the mission. You're to go to Los Angeles, California, to take part in an action movie that is being filmed in Hollywood."* Zak's ears had certainly perked up at that. *"The full details of your mission will be given to you by Assistant Director Reed when you arrive in the US. You will consider yourself under her command, but I need to be kept in the loop. I'm sending agent Wildcat with you – she has several years' more experience in the field than you, and she'll make sure everything runs smoothly."*

Zak had worked with Wildcat before. She was a year older than him, a lithe, lean girl with short spiky ash-blonde hair and a tendency to wear heavy black make-up around her eyes and black varnish on her nails.

The two of them had taken a flight to Washington the following day. A black limo had whisked them to the headquarters of the Federal Bureau of Investigation in Pennsylvania Avenue.

Assistant Director Isadora Reed was tall, tanned

and in command. She wore a stylish business suit and spoke with the tone of someone who was used to being obeyed. They'd been shown into a brightly lit office where the full details of their mission were spelled out to them.

"You're to watch this man," AD Reed told them, as a photo of a round-faced man in his mid-forties appeared on a wall-sized plasma screen. He had short, thinning hair and pale greenish eyes. He was wearing a tuxedo and there was a beautiful woman draped over his arm.

"His name is Elton Dean, and he owns and runs Parnassus Studios," AD Reed continued. "He's one of the more influential and wealthy movie producers in Hollywood. He lives here." She clicked on a small handheld device and the photo of a huge mansion appeared, surrounded by lawns and tennis courts and swimming pools, and all enclosed by a high stone wall.

"He is one of the producers behind an action movie called *Adrenaline Rush*. You'll be given all the information you need about the movie later. I'm in contact with the co-producers in New York, and it's through them that I've arranged for you two to be hired as stunt performers in the movie. I've also arranged for you to stay at Elton Dean's home in Beverley Hills. That will give you the perfect opportunity to keep him under close surveillance."

Zak didn't mind that at all. This was beginning to sound like a dream mission – flying to Hollywood, appearing in a movie, staying at a mansion in Beverley Hills. Way to be a spy!

"The reason you have a role in the movie, Quicksilver, is because the producers want to publicize *Adrenaline Rush* as a movie without CGI. A movie where what you see on the screen is real." She clicked again and the face of a very well-groomed boy of about Zak's age appeared. He was ridiculously good-looking, with bright blue eyes and high cheekbones.

"This is Scott Blaine, the actor playing the lead role. His character is an ordinary LA boy who suddenly finds he has super powers." She looked at Zak. "One of his powers is the ability to run ultra-fast. That's where you come in. You're going to do the running part of the stunt work for Scott. The movie people have been told that you're a budding British athlete, that your name is Zak Morrison and that you've been breaking records locally, but that you haven't made any appearances on the international track and field circuit yet." She turned to Wildcat. "You're his sister, Olivia. You're an Olympic-standard gymnast, but you've been dogged by injuries. It goes without saying that Dean and everyone else involved in the movie has no idea that you have any links with the FBI or British Intelligence."

And then they came to the heart of the mission – the reason why Elton Dean needed watching.

"The FBI has been tracking a terrorist commander who's known only by the codename Raging Moon," AD Reed explained. "Raging Moon has been behind several international atrocities in the past few years, and we have reason to believe he is on the western seaboard of the United States right now, busy hatching a new and imminent attack."

"A terrorist attack on America?" Zak asked.

"So far, our information isn't that specific," AD Reed replied. "All we know is that it's going to be big and it's going to happen soon. But we do have proof that Elton Dean has been in contact with Raging Moon."

"Elton Dean is part of a terrorist cell?" said Wildcat. "Why don't you just scoop him up and have done with it?"

"Because Dean isn't a terrorist," said AD Reed. "A few months back we found Dean had made a call to a phone number linked to Raging Moon. There was a tap on the phone line, and everything was recorded. The conversation was very brief and to the point, but it was clear Dean was agreeing to something that must have been discussed earlier. That set our antennae twitching and we started to dig through his entire life. There were no other terrorist links, but we *did* find some very shady financial dealings that went on right at the start of Dean's career. Long story short, Dean's empire is built on money he stole from his business partners when he was in his early twenties."

"Can't you arrest him for that?" Zak asked.

"We could," said AD Reed. "But then we'd lose our best hope of reeling in Raging Moon. Right now, our guess is that Raging Moon is using Dean's criminal past to blackmail him and force him to do what he wants."

"What would an international terrorist want from a movie producer?" asked Wildcat.

"I bet he's rich," said Zak. "Maybe Raging Moon wants money from him?"

"Possibly it is only that," said AD Reed. "But if I knew for sure what was going on, I wouldn't need you guys." She looked from one of them to the other. "Your mission is to get up close and personal with Dean and find out what Raging Moon wants from him. Once we know Dean's role in things, we should be able to figure out what Raging Moon is planning." She smiled coldly. "Then we'll have Raging Moon in the bag before he knows what hit him."

"And before his nasty plans come to the boil and innocent people get killed," added Wildcat.

"That's for sure," agreed AD Reed. "Okay, the two of you are booked on the fifteen-thirty flight out of Dulles Airport, due to land at LAX at twenty-fifty, local time. You'll be given some more background info on the flight, plus the full script of the movie. Do good work, guys – and keep me informed of your progress on a twice-daily basis."

Before they knew it, Zak and Wildcat had been on an aeroplane to Los Angeles, trying to get their heads around all the information they'd been loaded up with while flicking through the thick script of *Adrenaline Rush*.

Scott Blaine's character was a boy named Tyler McFadden. The first inkling Tyler McFadden had of his new powers was when he managed to outrun a speeding school bus full of little kids, jump aboard and bring the bus to a skidding halt.

Cue, Zak.

And cue the real-life murder of stunt driver Chet Blake, and the sabotage of the school bus.

Zak peered in the mirror and gave his hair a final tweak so that it stood up just the way he liked it. Then he stepped out of the small bathroom and joined Wildcat at the back of the trailer.

Her laptop was open on a low table. The screen was split between Assistant Director Reed's office in Washington, and the main briefing room in Fortress.

"Wildcat has been filling us in on what just happened," said AD Reed. "Is there any chance that bullet was intended for you and not the stuntman?"

"I don't think so," replied Zak. "He was dead before I even got on the bus." He was puzzled. "Why do you ask?"

"We were concerned that your cover might already be blown," said Colonel Hunter. "If someone knew an undercover British agent was on the film set, they might want to get rid of him."

Zak shook his head. "The police are sure the shot came from a high-powered rifle fired from a rooftop about a thousand metres away from the bus. They think they know the exact building the gunman was on. They worked it out from the angle of the shot."

"That means the rifle was in the hands of someone who knew what they were doing," added Wildcat. "If they'd wanted to shoot Silver, they wouldn't have missed."

"I think you're right," said AD Reed. "The gunman got

the guy he meant to hit. Do the police have anything on who messed with the bus?"

"They've interviewed the mechanics," said Wildcat. "It seems that there were two guys in the garage where the bus was kept that no one remembers seeing before."

"Bad security," growled Colonel Hunter. "I assume they've disappeared?"

"That's right," said Zak. "Apparently everyone thought someone else knew who they were. No one double-checked the bus before the shoot began."

"I'm in contact with the LA Chief of Police," said AD Reed. "If they come up with anything useful, I'll let you know. But my take on this is that it was a professional hit – the gunman and the bogus mechanics will be long gone by now."

"What was the purpose of killing the stunt driver and tampering with the bus?" asked Colonel Hunter.

"I'll have to take a rain check on that one, Peter," said AD Reed. "But that's where Quicksilver and Wildcat come in. They can do some sniffing around."

"Agreed," said the Colonel. "But keep it low-key – the last thing we need is for people to get suspicious of the two of you this early on. Maybe the incident has something to do with Elton Dean's relationship with Raging Moon, but there's also the chance that it's entirely unconnected."

"We're on it, Control," said Zak.

"Wildcat told us how you stayed on the bus and saved Dean's nephew," said AD Reed. "Way to go, Quicksilver. You're the hero of the hour."

The smile that began to form on Zak's face was quickly wiped away by Colonel Hunter's stern expression. "I'd expect no less from any of my agents, Assistant Director," he said. His eyes met Zak's and he gave the smallest of nods. "Vid-link terminated."

The Colonel vanished from the screen. That nod was enough for Zak. It meant he'd done well.

"A hard man to impress," said AD Reed. "Still, kudos on you, Quicksilver. Honour is due. Get in touch if you have anything to report. We'll talk soon." The screen went blank. Wildcat leaned forwards and shut the laptop.

She gave Zak a sidelong look. "You know Control is proud of what you did, don't you?" she said.

"Of course," Zak replied. He grinned. "*Honour is due*? What does that even mean?"

Wildcat rolled her eyes. "How about: *kudos on you*?" She got up. "Don't you just love America?" She walked to the door. "Come on, let's go and see what's happening out there. Things should have calmed down a little by now."

✳

The chaos that had erupted in the immediate aftermath of the incident had certainly died down. The traumatized kids had been taken home, except for one or two with cuts and bruises who had been ferried to the nearest hospital to be checked over.

Firefighters had put out the blazing bus. Now it was standing in a lake of filthy water, blackened, burnt out, and slimy with muddy ash from where the hoses had played on it. An ambulance had taken Chet Blake's body away in a black bag.

Whoever had set this whole thing up clearly had no concern for human life. If Zak hadn't been there . . . well, he didn't want to think about that.

Zak had already made an initial statement to the police, but they wanted him to go along to the local station later that afternoon to give them a full blow-by-blow account.

All the movie-making gear was still around; the crew looked shell-shocked, people were either gathered in small groups, talking quietly, or being interviewed by the dozen or so police officers who were still on site.

The whole road was cordoned off with yellow tape. CRIME SCENE. DO NOT CROSS. Police crime scene analysts in white coveralls with hoods and face masks were scouring the whole area, searching for every scrap of forensic evidence.

Zak wasn't sure they'd find anything. As Assistant Director Reed had said, it looked as though professionals had done this. They weren't about to leave evidence lying around.

TV crews had gathered at the end of the road, kept back by an armed SWAT team but aiming their cameras and mikes up the hill in the hope of gleaning some little scrap of news. There was a news helicopter buzzing about overhead.

Zak spotted Elton Dean and Grayson Clarke with the Commander of the local Police Operational Bureau and some other high-ranking police officers. Elton Dean was a rich and powerful man – the big guns had been called out.

Elton Dean looked shaken and scared. *No surprise there*, thought Zak. His nephew had almost been killed. Various assistants swarmed around him, some speaking on phones, others tapping at Blackberries.

"I'll go and mingle with the crew," said Wildcat. "See if anyone is saying anything interesting."

She headed off and Zak walked towards Elton Dean and the others. Grayson Clarke had moved away from them, and was talking into his mobile phone. "Yes, I do know how much money this delay is costing, Mr

Wiseman. I intend to get the movie back on track as soon as possible." He was red-faced with annoyance and frustration. "A man is dead, Mr Wiseman. I know you and your fellow producers are concerned about your investment, but some delay is inevitable after a tragedy like this." Zak guessed he was talking to one of the New York co-producers that Assistant Director Reed had mentioned. It was pretty obvious that the businessmen in New York were more concerned about their money than about a dead stunt driver.

He moved closer to Elton Dean and the Police Commander. Zak could see the sweat running down Elton Dean's face. His voice sounded pretty shaky too.

"I want you to do a thorough job, Commander, but you have to understand we're running to tight schedules," Elton Dean was saying. "All I'm asking is that you finish as quickly as possible." He glanced at his wristwatch. "I have to host a very important function in four hours. I really don't have the time to stand here answering the same questions over and over."

"You're still intending to hold the party at your house, Mr Dean?" asked the Commander, sounding surprised. "After what's happened here today?"

Elton Dean looked at the Commander. "I certainly am," he said. "Have you any idea how difficult it is to organize something that big? There are people flying in from all over. I have bands ready to perform. I have caterers for five hundred people. I have one hundred bottles of Dom Pérignon Reserve on ice." He frowned. "Listen, if you want my opinion, this whole thing was set up by a disgruntled ex-employee out for revenge. You don't get rich around here without upsetting a few people. Do you know how many enemies I have in this town?"

Without waiting for a reply, he marched off, his assistants streaming along behind him. He passed Zak, hardly giving him a glance. At first he'd wanted to blame Zak for the whole thing. It was only when it had become clear that Chet Blake had been shot and the bus had been tampered with that he'd reluctantly accepted that Zak had saved a disaster from happening. Even then he hadn't bothered to thank Zak for saving his nephew and all those other kids. Dean was clearly upset and agitated by the incident, but mainly he just seemed anxious to limit the delay in the shoot.

Zak saw the Commander shake his head and close his notebook. He turned to the officers at his back. "You heard the man," he said. "Let's wrap it up – Mr Dean has a *party* to attend."

Zak watched as Elton Dean climbed into a waiting white Lincoln Stretch limousine. One by one, his assistants piled in after him, vanishing behind the tinted windows.

The limousine glided away, leaving Zak staring after it. He decided he didn't much like Elton Dean. He guessed he wasn't the only one.

CHAPTER **THREE**

THE PARNASSUS MANSION, BEVERLEY HILLS, CALIFORNIA.

Elton Dean's home was huge and luxurious with wings leading off in all directions. It was entirely surrounded by paved courtyards and clipped lawns and swimming pools and koi carp ponds. Inside, it was stuffed with exotic antiques from just about every country in the world.

Zak was up in his second floor bedroom, getting ready for the big party. Looking out of the window, he could see Elton Dean had spared no expense to make his party the talk of Hollywood.

Coloured lasers were strobing the sky, pulsing to the rhythm of remixed dance hits. Rainbow lanterns hung in loops along the pathways. There were two outdoor kitchens, as well as a small funfair out on one of the lawns where a merry-go-round spun and a big wheel churned around and a dozen sideshows blazed with lights.

"Could Elton Dean be more of a show-off?" said Zak, watching as the first glamorous guests began to arrive.

"He's overcompensating," Wildcat said, sitting in an armchair. "He probably didn't have enough toys when he was a kid."

Zak was wearing a suit. He wasn't a big fan of suits, but he'd been told the party was a "coat and tie" affair, which Cat had translated as meaning he had to look smart. She was in a little black dress and not quite so much of her trademark dark eye make-up as usual.

"Where have you put the gadgets?" Wildcat asked.

"They're in my bedside drawer," Zak replied. "We won't need them tonight, will we?"

Colonel Hunter had supplied them with some special Project 17 devices. A pair of sunglasses, a small black rubber ball about the size of a table tennis ball, a pack of chewing gum, a small box of dental floss and a very unusual click-top ballpoint pen. None of them was quite what they seemed to be, and at the appropriate time, Zak was looking forward to trying them all out.

"I don't think so," said Wildcat. "Even if we get spotted, the worst that can happen is we'll be told off for being in places we shouldn't." She looked Zak up and down. "Zingy!" she said. "Ready to go down and mingle?"

Zak nodded.

Mingling with Elton Dean's guests was only part of what they had planned. The party was the perfect diversion. It was time to move the mission on. First of all, they'd go and join the fun, then each of them would slip quietly away while the other covered for them.

They had some private rooms to search.

"Look!" Cat whispered in Zak's ear for maybe the fifteenth time so far that evening. "See who it is?" She was gesturing furtively towards a tall, drop-dead-gorgeous woman in a gold dress.

"No. Who is it?"

"Paige Thoreau. You know. From the TV show, *Spindrift.*"

"Never heard of her. Never watched the show. Never

will," said Zak. He was quite enjoying pretending not to recognize people – it drove Cat wild trying to explain that he *must* know them. *Everyone* knows them!

Zak was playing it cool to wind up Cat, but he was actually having a pretty good time, star-spotting and rubbing shoulders with the kinds of people you only normally saw supersized on a movie screen, or as tiny dots on the stage of an arena rock concert.

He'd noticed a few of the people from *Adrenaline Rush* about the place – Scott Blaine, the actor playing the hero Tyler McFadden, was there, along with several other actors he'd seen on set. Grayson Clarke had turned up with a beautiful woman on each arm and Elton Dean was parading around, doing his best to behave as if nothing bad had happened that day.

Zak and Cat had been at the party for about an hour now. It was large and loud and overwhelming. The noise of the chattering guests almost drowned out the music and almost everyone seemed to have a champagne glass permanently in their hand. There was one main topic of conversation, despite Elton Dean's determination to ignore it. And that was the death of Chet Blake and the near-fatal incident with the bus load of kids.

Assistant Director Reed had been right. Zak was treated as a hero. Some people wanted to say hello or to be photographed with him, others wanted to hear all the details of the rescue. In fact, Zak was so in demand that he was beginning to wonder if he'd ever get the opportunity to disappear the way he and Cat had planned.

His chance came when an announcement boomed out over the loudspeaker system.

"Ladies and gentlemen, would you please assemble on the front terrace, where our special guest performers BlingBamBoom are about to go on stage!"

The mega-selling girl band were riding high in the charts right now with their hit song "Want It, Take It, Own It". Everyone was desperate for a piece of the action, so having them perform at a private party was a really big deal.

Buzzing with excitement, the guests began to swarm towards the big patio at the front of the house where the stage had been set up. Wildcat joined the crowd while Zak slipped quietly away through a side door.

He tucked himself behind a curtain, waiting for the last few people to leave. He heard applause and cheering, then some heavy dance beats kicked in. The show was on.

Elton Dean had his own permanent security guards – four or five beefy guys whose job it was to patrol the mansion and its grounds. That was why the party was such a great diversion. With any luck, the guards would be too busy watching the guests outside to worry about checking upstairs too often.

Zak stepped from cover and jogged across to a staircase. He went up it in long four-step lopes. He looked at his Mob, a smartphone used by British Intelligence. It brought up a floor plan of the mansion so he would be able to find the rooms he wanted.

Elton Dean had a suite of private rooms and offices on the second floor at the back of the main building. Zak's job was to search the offices, then go back to the party and cover for Wildcat while she went through Dean's other rooms. They had no specific idea of what they were looking for. AD Reed and Colonel Hunter wanted some concrete proof of the link between Elton Dean and Raging Moon. So, documents, desk diaries, computer files, if the password needed to access them wasn't too complex.

In a secret little pocket under his belt, Zak had a memory stick given to him by Bug, Project 17's electronics uber-nerd. There was a Trojan Horse program on it that could crack any ordinary passwords. It also had a nifty little file that was able to wipe any indication that the computer had been hacked. Bug had told them to download anything interesting or suspicious and mail it to him from Wildcat's laptop.

Another flight of stairs and a couple of corridors later, Zak was standing at the door to Elton Dean's office. The door was protected by a keypad. Press four digits and enter.

Zak held his Mob up and took a picture of the keypad. He ran the photo through a smart little app that was designed to show fingerprint impressions. The numbers 1, 2, 7 and 0 revealed constant use. There were only twenty-four permutations of the four numbers. Zak got it right on the third attempt.

He slipped into the room and closed the door behind him. He took out his pencil torch and roved the beam around the room, avoiding the windows. The walls were covered in framed photographs of Elton Dean with movie stars and politicians and other well-groomed, smiling people that Zak didn't recognize.

He walked towards a huge mahogany desk where a few movie awards were displayed. There was even an Oscar! *Not bad.*

There was also a slimline computer. Zak moved behind the desk, the pencil torch between his teeth as he went carefully through various piles of documents. Mostly it seemed to be movie scripts and contracts and stuff like that. Not what he was looking for.

He tapped the keyboard and the computer screen lit up to show a photo of Elton Dean shaking hands with the President of the United States.

Oh, please. Would you like to show off just a little bit more?

A box opened on screen asking for a password. Zak slid the memory stick into a USB port and waited. A sub-page opened and number and letters began to scroll down as Bug's device tried to find the password to let Zak into the computer.

He perched on the edge of the chair, checking out the desk while he waited. There was one of those large old-fashioned leather blotters under the keyboard. The corner of a white sheet of paper poked out from beneath it, as though it had been shoved out of sight – but not quite well enough.

Zak tugged it. It wasn't a sheet of paper at all – it was an envelope. It was pretty mangled, as though it had been ripped open either by someone in a bad mood or in a rush to know what was inside.

Zak took out the single folded sheet of paper and smoothed it on the desk. Almost filling the page was an odd drawing. It was a stylized depiction of a snake, drawn in a circle with the tip of its tail in its mouth.

Inside the hoop made by the snake, someone had scribbled a message in capital letters.

THAT WAS A REMINDER. NEXT TIME MORE PEOPLE WILL DIE.

Startled, Zak examined the torn envelope again. It was addressed:

Elton Dean – Private & Confidential

Printed. There was no actual address and no postmark or stamps.

"Hand-delivered," Zak murmured. "*Next time more people will die.*" He frowned, watching the letter and numbers spinning past on the computer screen as Bug's Trojan Horse tried to find the password. No luck so far. But his mind was busy with the scribble in the snake-ring. There was only one interpretation for that message.

It had to refer to the incident at the shoot.

A reminder. A reminder from whom? A reminder to do what?

Zak took a couple of pictures with his Mob then folded the paper back into the envelope and pushed it under the blotter again.

He stared impatiently at the screen. "Come on," he muttered. "Get on with it."

A sound from beyond the office door put Zak on instant high alert. It was a voice. No. Two voices. Straying partygoers looking for a bathroom? They'd need to have got themselves very lost to be up here.

Then he heard the beeping noise of someone punching the pass-code into the keypad outside the door.

Uh oh! Time's up.

Zak snatched the memory stick from the USB port and switched off his torch. He clicked on the icon top left of the computer screen, putting it into sleep mode. The screen went dark.

Zak slipped out of the chair, intending to lie low under the desk. But the chair creaked loudly just as the office door opened from outside.

"Did you hear that?" asked a sharp voice.

"What?" answered another. Male voices. Not partygoer voices. Security guard voices.

"I heard something. Stay here, I'm going to check it out."

Zak glanced over his shoulder. There was a window behind the desk.

Speed, don't fail me now!

He dived for the window, yanking the catch down and giving the frame a hefty shove. The window swung open. Zak sprang onto the sill.

He heard a shout. "Stop! Stop right there!"

No time to think things through. No time to think at all. Spreading his arms, Zak launched himself off the window sill.

CHAPTER **FOUR**

The security guard ran to the window. All he'd seen was a shadow – a black shape, framed for a split second before jumping. He leaned out. Beneath the window stretched a wide striped awning. It was shaking from where someone had landed and slid down. Beyond the awning the guard could see the far side of one of Mr Dean's koi carp ponds. The water was sloshing about, but the interloper had dropped out of sight.

The second guard slapped the light on.

The man at the window spun around. "He went out this way. Get downstairs. Alert the others," he barked.

The second man vanished from the room. The first guard stared around. Checking for signs of the intrusion. No. Nothing obvious. He went to the desk and woke up the computer. He typed rapidly, his eyes narrowed.

A page came up in response.

All Clear.

Good. No sign that the password had been cracked. Shutting the device down again, he headed for the door. He'd told Mr Dean there should be added security during the party. All those bodies about the place, all those greedy fingers and peering eyes. It was asking for trouble. It was like sitting up and begging for it.

ONE MINUTE EARLIER.

Zak landed feet first on the wide canvas awning. He tucked his head in and used the momentum of his fall to curl into a forward roll. He grabbed the bottom edge of the awning and turned head over heels, straightening himself out and preparing to hit the ground and run for it before Elton Dean's goons could see a thing.

How great an escape was that? And the awning had

been the cherry on the cake. Without it, a jump from a second floor window would have meant a broken ankle, or worse. Now all he needed to do was slip around to the front and lose himself in the crowd.

Except that instead of landing on solid ground, he came splashing down into a metre of water. The gravelly ground shifted under his feet. He lost his balance and toppled backwards. Cold water engulfed him. Spluttering, he rose to the surface and clawed his way to the stone lip of the koi carp pond.

Way to go, Zak. Never heard of "look before you leap"?

He got to his feet, his suit streaming with water and his hair dripping in his eyes. At least the awning hid him from view of the window. Pulling weedy fronds off his jacket, Zak squelched across the paved walkway.

Now what? He needed to get to his room, dry off and find some clothes to change into. All without being seen.

He pushed through some French windows and made his way across a darkened room. He took his Mob out of his pocket. On a previous mission, one of his Mobs had been ruined when it had been dumped in a sink full of water. Since then, the white-coats at Project 17 had come up with a waterproof casing.

Zak pressed the pad at the base of the Mob and the screen lit.

Well, at least now he could tell them that the casing had been field-tested.

He opened the door out of the room and came face-to-face with one of Elton Dean's security guards.

They stared at one another for a few seconds. Zak wasn't sure which of them was more startled.

"Follow me, young man," said the guard.

Zak nodded, doing his best to look ashamed and guilty. He didn't say anything. He had to play this carefully. He didn't want to come off as too sure of himself. He had to act like an ordinary kid caught doing something he shouldn't have.

The guard led him through the mansion to the big reception area behind the main doors. The walls were lined with buffet tables, but the place was empty of guests. BlingBamBoom were still playing outside. But Elton Dean was there, standing at the bottom of a long sweeping staircase, talking to a woman in a bright red dress.

"Wait here, son," the guard told him. He left Zak dripping in the middle of the floor while he went over to Elton Dean and whispered in his ear.

Zak knew exactly what Elton Dean was being told, and his mind was working fast to try and come up with an alternative explanation.

The woman turned, looking him up and down. Her red

lipstick smile widened as she walked over to where he was standing. First impression. Late thirties? Personal-trainer slim. Immaculate make-up. Salon-cut, long tumbling flame-red hair, green eyes, red lips, a red party dress and high red stilettos. A woman who took a lot of time over her appearance.

"You're Zak Morrison, aren't you?" she said. "The hero of the hour. My name's Bree Van Hausen. I'm CEO of the Los Angeles branch of the Worldwide Synergy public relations conglomerate." She paused for a moment. "You're wet."

"Yes," he said, watching Elton Dean and the guard over her shoulder. "Yes, I am."

"Are they playing some kind of water game out there?" she asked.

"No," said Zak. "I did this all by myself. I fell in a fish pond."

Her smile almost split her face in half. "I just love your cute accent, Zak. I can use that – people will adore you."

He blinked at her. "I'm sorry . . . *what*?"

"Listen, Zak, Elton has hired me and my company to oversee the publicity for *Adrenaline Rush*," Bree Van Hausen began. "That was a total tragedy today with the bus and everything, but there's an old saying in the world of public relations. There's no such thing as bad publicity – and if the world gives you lemons, make lemonade."

Zak stared at her. She was obviously nuts, but he assumed she was telling him this for a reason.

"The thing is, Zak, your heroics today will make great copy for the movie," she said. "People love a real-life hero and when they know you were actually involved in the movie too, it'll increase the audience figures at the opening weekend by fifty or sixty per cent, according to my provisional survey figures." She looked at him closely, still smiling. "I have some great ideas for how you can make the most of the news cycle while you're still hot property. Talk shows, live interviews, the whole nine yards. You'll be a celebrity. Everyone in the entire world will know your face, Zak, all the way from New York to LA. How's that sound?"

"Ummm . . ." Zak was trying to think of a polite way to tell her that he'd rather be found dead in a drain than appear on a talk show. As if Colonel Hunter would allow that to happen anyway. "I'm not sure . . ."

"Everyone wants to be a star, Zak," Bree Van Hausen insisted. "Here's the thing. I can see you're a guy who likes to make up his own mind." She dug her red-nailed fingers into a red handbag and produced a red card with white writing. "All my details are on here. Promise me you'll think about it, Zak. What say we do lunch at my office? No strings attached. I can lay out some alternative strategies to maximize your potential, and you can ask me all the questions that occur to you." She moved closer, holding his eyes, her voice persuasive. "Will you do that for me at least? Lunch at my office?"

"Yes," said Zak, feeling uncomfortable. "That'll be fine."

"Outstanding!" she said. "I'll have my secretary set the whole thing up."

Zak nodded, feeling as if he'd been in a hurricane.

Elton Dean strode towards him. "I'd like a word with this young man, if you'd be good enough to let us have the room, Bree," he said.

"I'll catch you later," Bree Van Hausen said to Zak. "Toodles!" She swept away, leaving Zak and Elton Dean standing and looking at one another.

"Brad tells me that someone was seen in my office a few minutes ago," said Elton Dean, gesturing to the guard, who was standing a few metres away with a stony expression on his face. Elton Dean's eyes narrowed. "An uninvited guest in my private office. He went out of the window. Landed in one of my ponds." He looked pointedly at Zak's saturated clothing. "Have you been upstairs, Zak?"

Zak made his eyes as wide as saucers. "So he was a burglar, was he?" he gasped. "I just thought he was one of your party guests who'd had too much champagne.

Wow! I suppose I should have yelled for help, but it all happened so quickly."

A puzzled expression came over Elton Dean's face. "What are you talking about?"

"I was around the back, looking at your koi carp," Zak began. "I love the really colourful ones. Did you know that people in China have been keeping koi carp for over a thousand years? Apparently they bred them selectively so . . ."

"Never mind the koi carp," interrupted Elton Dean. "What's this about a burglar?"

"Like I said," Zak continued breathlessly. "I was checking out the koi in your pond when some big guy suddenly dropped right on top of me from the awning. He knocked me into the pond!" He did his best to sound a little on the scatty side. "I couldn't believe it! He didn't say sorry or anything. He just ran off across the lawn towards the wall."

Elton Dean stared at him for a few long seconds. Zak couldn't tell if he was buying the story or not. "What did he look like?" he asked at last.

"He was dressed in black." Zak paused for a moment, as though trying to recall details. "Oh! And he had a scar down his right cheek." He traced a line down his own face. "Just like that. A big, ugly scar."

"Would you describe him as a large man?" asked Elton Dean.

"Pretty large," agreed Zak. "Look, I'm dripping all over your floor. I really need to go and change."

"You do that, Zak," said Elton Dean. "And if you remember anything else about the man, you'll tell me, won't you?"

"Of course," said Zak, already heading for the stairs.

He gave the glowering guard a quick smile as he passed. He forced himself not to look back as he climbed the stairs. The innocent act had to be faultless if it was going to work.

At the top of the stairs, he risked the briefest of glances down. Elton Dean and the guard were huddled together. Dean was talking and the guard was shaking his head. At the last moment before Zak moved out of sight, Elton Dean looked up at him.

It was a look filled with suspicion.

Half an hour later Zak had showered and managed to find a reasonable change of clothes so he could rejoin the party. BlingBamBoom were taking a break and the audience had spread out again over the grounds of the Parnassus Mansion. Some people were lining up at the barbecues and mobile sushi bars for food; others were making the most of the fairground attractions. The rest stood around drinking and talking.

Fortunately, Zak was no longer the centre of attention. He and Wildcat managed to find a quiet corner to exchange information. There was plenty to talk about.

"We'll have to be ten times more careful now," Wildcat murmured as they sat next to each other on a low wall. "You think he believed your story about the burglar?"

"Hard to tell," said Zak. "I *think* I got away with it. I'm pretty sure he has me down as an idiot, though."

"That's good," said Wildcat. "Stupid is good, under the circumstances." She shook her head. "But you shouldn't have agreed to meet up with that Bree Van Hausen woman. All those ideas she has about making you famous? That can't happen. Colonel Hunter would go ballistic."

"I know," said Zak. "I got cornered into 'doing lunch' with her, but I can back out of it, no problem."

"Everyone in America is desperate to get on TV," said Wildcat. "We need a convincing reason why you aren't up for it. We can run it past AD Reed and Control – they'll think of something."

"I wish I'd had more time with the computer," said Zak. "I didn't get a thing out of it. And I don't suppose we're going to be given a second chance."

"No," said Wildcat. "That would be too big a risk." She frowned. "But I'm intrigued by that warning you found." She looked at the photo on Zak's Mob.

THAT WAS A REMINDER. NEXT TIME MORE PEOPLE WILL DIE.

"The design rings a bell," Wildcat murmured. "A snake eating its own tail. I'm sure I've seen it before, but I can't remember where or when."

"Are you still planning to scope out Elton Dean's rooms, or should we call it a day?" asked Zak. "They'll be on high alert now."

Wildcat looked thoughtful. "I'm not so sure," she said. "If they bought your story about the burglar, they'll think he's gone. And even if they suspect you were up to no good in Dean's office, they'd have their eye on you, not me." She stood up. "I'm going to give it a shot," she said. "If I think I'm being watched, I'll act stupid and lost."

"Brother and sister act," Zak said with a slight smile. "Tweedledum and Tweedle-even-more-dumb!"

"Oh, indeed," said Wildcat with a wink. "And I know which is which." She glanced around. No one was paying them any attention. "Okay, it's show time, brother of mine. If anyone asks for me, I've gone to the bathroom. Tell them I think I ate some dodgy prawns so I might be a while."

"Got it." Zak looked up at her, his face serious. "Cat?"

"What?"

"Be careful," Zak said. "Those security guards look pretty tough."

Wildcat grinned. "So am I, Silver, my friend," she said. "So am I."

CHAPTER **FIVE**

Wildcat had a few close encounters on her way up to Elton Dean's private rooms. Security guards were definitely on the prowl, but she knew how to keep out of sight. Searching a room without leaving a trace was something Project 17 agents were taught from very early on. On entering a room, first of all check your exit strategies and potential hiding places. Use your eyes more than your hands. Put things back exactly the way you found them. Give nothing away.

Wildcat searched Elton Dean's bedroom and en-suite bathroom quickly but expertly, using a pencil torch to light her way. There was nothing out of the ordinary. Nothing to link the millionaire movie producer to the terrorist threat.

Disappointing.

If only Quicksilver had had enough time to get some stuff off the computer. Still, they weren't out of options yet. They'd nail him. They hadn't travelled halfway around the world to give up now.

She padded out of the room and made her way along the corridor. The door to Elton Dean's office was open a fraction. She could hear his voice from inside. She paused, glancing both ways, then she moved closer to the door and listened.

"I don't care what you say, there is something screwy about that Brit kid," he was saying. There was a pause.

He was obviously talking to someone on the telephone.

"No, I don't know for sure it was him in my office," he continued. "He gave me some story about a man with a scar. Said the guy ran for the wall. But I've had my people check it out and there's no sign anyone got out that way."

So Elton Dean hadn't *entirely* believed Quicksilver's tale.

"No, I don't know why he'd be in my office. Maybe he

wanted a souvenir of his stay here. Or perhaps he was hoping to hack my computer and—" His voice stopped abruptly. He must have been interrupted by the person on the other end of the line. "I get that, but listen to me," Elton Dean continued after a few moments. "The bottom line is, I don't trust the kid. He should be let go, that's all I'm saying." Another pause. "Send him and his sister back to England and get a couple of replacements." Another longer pause. "I am not paranoid. I know you people in New York think he's great for publicity, with that speed thing he has going for him, but . . ." Yet another long pause. She could hear Elton Dean breathing hard. He must be speaking to one of the co-producers Assistant Director Reed had mentioned. She had said they were from New York.

"Okay, okay," he said at last. "I'll hold off on any decision for the time being, but I'm telling you, that kid is bad news. Wait . . . I have another call coming through. I'll have to get back to you." There was a moment of silence before Elton Dean began speaking again. This time there was a remarkable difference in his tone of voice. It sounded as if he was speaking to someone he was afraid of. "Yes," he said. "I'm sorry, I tried, but they're not buying it. Of course I did – but those New York guys are funding seventy per cent of the movie – what they say goes, and they want the boy to stay." Pause. "Yes, I do know what's at stake. Believe me, after what happened today, you don't have to worry about me not following through, okay?"

Wildcat held her breath. This was far more interesting. He was talking to someone who frightened him – someone linked to the incident with the shooting of Chet Blake and the near disaster with the school bus. Who was he talking to? Raging Moon himself, perhaps?

She heard a sound from the far end of the hall. Someone was coming. She swore under her breath as she slipped silently away.

PACIFIC STANDARD TIME (LOS ANGELES): 01:27.
GREENWICH MEAN TIME (LONDON): 09:27.

The party was over.

Zak and Cat were in her room, sitting on the bed with the laptop propped open in front of them. The screen was split again, between the FBI field office in Wilshire Boulevard, Los Angeles and the main briefing room in Fortress.

Assistant Director Reed and Colonel Hunter had been

brought up to speed on that evening's events.

"Wildcat is quite correct," Colonel Hunter said. "We can't allow Quicksilver to appear on television – our agreement with the FBI was based on the fact that his face would never be seen."

"I'm afraid the ship has sailed on that one, Peter," said AD Reed. "The incident yesterday with the bus and the homicide is big news, at least on the Western Seaboard."

"I understand that, Assistant Director," said the Colonel. "But we need to do some damage limitation now. Quicksilver has to get out of the public gaze as quickly as possible."

"Though like I said," added Wildcat. "Everyone here is desperate to get on TV – how do we back away without making it look weird?"

"I think I have a solution," said AD Reed. "I'm going to put it out on the grapevine that Mr Morrison here has signed an exclusive contract with one of the major Hollywood talent agencies. The whisper will be that they have full rights over him, and they don't want him appearing anywhere till they've had time to do some cosmetic surgery. We'll suggest he needs extensive dental work, for a start. As he's British, the media will buy that, no problem."

"Excuse me," interrupted Zak, offended. "What's that

supposed to mean?"

"Chill out, Silver," said Cat with a smile. "It only means you don't have expensive movie-star teeth."

"I'll leave you to organize that, Assistant Director," said Colonel Hunter. "As for that design found on the warning note to Mr Dean, I've had Bug do some digging. Let him tell you what he's discovered." The Colonel's face was replaced on screen by the heavily fringed face of the twelve-year-old computer genius known as Bug.

"The design is called the Ouroboros," Bug began, not pausing to say hello. "In the old days, the symbol of the snake or serpent eating its own tail was meant to represent the circle of life, but it also has a secondary meaning to do with the clash of opposites."

"Run that past me again, Bug?" asked AD Reed.

"Good and bad, light and dark," said Bug. "That kind of thing. The serpent eating its own tail is sometimes thought to be a symbol of evil eating good. The design is also known as the Worm Ouroboros – the word 'worm' meaning snake or dragon. Or it can be referred to as the world serpent."

"Is that a fact?" murmured AD Reed. "Well, now."

"So, where does that get us?" asked Wildcat.

"Hold on," said Zak, sitting up suddenly. "I know that from somewhere."

"You know what, Quicksilver?" asked AD Reed.

"World serpent," said Zak. "I've heard it before."

Colonel Hunter's voice had a sharp edge to it. "When and where?" he asked.

"I can't remember," said Zak, frowning as he tried to pinpoint the hazy memory.

"Interesting," said AD Reed. "Peter? Is there something you need to tell me?"

"There's nothing, Assistant Director, I can assure you," said Colonel Hunter. His gaze flickered from Zak to Cat. "Take no risks, agents," he said. "Keep a watching brief on Elton Dean, but do nothing that might provoke his suspicions further. The last thing we want is for him to take you off the movie."

"Agreed," said AD Reed. "If that second call Dean took this evening was from someone linked to the terrorists, then Raging Moon may already know what happened in his office. Elton Dean being suspicious of Zak is one thing – a bunch of terrorists thinking the same is a whole other ballpark."

"Be smart, be safe," said Colonel Hunter. "And keep me in the loop."

"We need a word, Peter," said AD Reed.

"I know we do," said the Colonel. "I'll call you on a private line. Fortress out." The screen flipped so that only AD Reed's face could be seen.

"Watch your backs, guys," said the Assistant Director. "These creeps play hardball, remember that."

Then she was gone.

Wildcat leaned forwards and closed the laptop. "Did it get weird between the two of them towards the end?" she asked.

Zak nodded. "After I said I'd heard of world serpent before," he agreed. "I wonder what the problem was."

"Something way above our pay grade, I guess," said Wildcat. "Okay, I don't know about you, but I'm worn out. And we have an early call in the morning, don't forget."

"Oh, yes," said Zak, climbing off her bed and heading for his own room. "The next location shoot. Where is it again?"

"Malibu Beach," said Wildcat. "If I'm going to be nearly drowned, I'll need my best bikini."

The crazy, chaotic trappings of the *Adrenaline Rush* location shoot descended on Malibu Beach early next morning. They were in a place called Paradise Cove. The entire area had been hired for the day and all the trailers and trucks were parked on a wide stretch of concrete next to a beachfront restaurant.

Wildcat and Zak stood on the long sandy beach, watching the ocean rollers tumbling in. Exclusive beach houses lay half-hidden by trees all along the seafront, and more could be glimpsed where the ground rose into steep, forested hills and brown cliffs.

A couple of people had already sidled up to Zak and asked him which of the Hollywood talent agencies he had signed with. Assistant Director Reed's rumour campaign was clearly working. Zak simply smiled and said he wasn't allowed to talk about it.

The film crews were swarming over the beach, setting up their equipment ready for the filming to begin. A truck had been driven down to the shoreline with a camera crane mounted on its back. A couple of men with heavy-looking Steadicams were also down there, getting ready to climb into boats. A bunch of extras were gathered together and being given instructions by a couple of assistants.

Grayson Clarke was speaking to Scott Blaine, his arms waving to and fro as he explained the details of the shoot to the young actor. Not that Scott would be doing a whole lot of acting today. He was there for the close-ups. When it came to the real action, they'd be calling on Zak again.

"I have to pretend I can't swim," Cat said, as the two

of them sat high on the beach, out of everyone's way and reading through their scripts again. "It says here: *Tyler McFadden races down the beach. He plunges into the water, regardless of his own safety and swims at super-speed towards the three beautiful girls who are floundering helplessly in the ocean.*" Cat looked at him. "Exactly how fast can you swim, Silver?"

He looked at her. "Exactly, how *beautiful* are you, Cat?"

"To die for," said Cat, raising her eyebrows. "And the swimming?"

"I can swim okay, for someone my age, apparently," Zak said. "When I first joined Project 17, Dr Jackson did some swimming tests on me." Dr Jackson was one of Colonel Hunter's top scientists. "My adrenaline thing doesn't make much difference in water apparently." Zak shrugged. "Dr Jackson said it was something to do with water having a higher density than air."

Cat nodded. "And salt water is even denser that fresh water," she said. "Fresh water has a density of one, and seawater has a density of one point zero two five."

Zak gave her a sidelong glance. Sometimes he forgot how brainy she was. "I told Mr Clarke that I couldn't swim super-fast and he just said they'd fix it in post-production," he told her. "I suppose they'll do it with some kind of special effects."

"I thought the whole point of this movie was that they wouldn't be using any special effects," said Cat.

Zak nodded. "That's what I said, but Mr Clarke just laughed and shook his head as if I was being especially dim." He flipped through the script pages. "There's a scene later on where they blow up the Hollywood sign. That'll be cool."

"No way are they doing that for real," said Cat.

"Did you read it all the way to the end?" Zak asked.

"Where a gang of bank robbers take over a water pumping station and threaten to blow it up?" said Wildcat. "Yes, I read it." She shook her head. "It didn't make much sense. Okay, so the police moved in on the gang as they were coming out of the bank with bags of loot. There was a big shoot-out, and then a car chase when the gang tried to escape."

"That's right," said Zak. "The gang drives up into the hills and ends up at one of the main pumping stations along the Los Angeles Aqueduct. They rig a bomb to blow the whole place sky high, then demand a huge ransom not to set the bomb off, a helicopter to take them to the nearest airport and a plane on the runway to fly them out of the country."

"That's fine, but where did the bomb come from?" Wildcat asked.

Zak shook his head. "Typical girl," he said. "You didn't read it properly, did you? They have the bomb making stuff with them because they thought they might need it to get into the bank vault. In the end the bank manager gives them the combination to the vault, so they didn't have to use it – but it was in the getaway car all along."

Wildcat made a non-committal grunting noise. "How very convenient for them," she muttered.

Zak smiled. "It's a *movie*," he reminded her.

"Does that mean it shouldn't need to make sense?" asked Wildcat.

"It makes sense to me," said Zak.

"Yes, well, you're a boy," Cat said scathingly. "As long as stuff keeps getting blown up, boys don't care so much about plots."

"You got that right," Zak said with a laugh. "Oh!" He pointed down the beach. "I think she's looking for you."

It was Marnie, one of Grayson Clarke's little assistants. She was plodding up the sand, clutching a clipboard and looking flustered.

"Hi, Olivia," she panted. "Mr Grayson needs you for your cue now." She pointed down the beach to where a small motor boat had been drawn up in the tumbling surf. "You and Kelly and Maple need to be ready in plenty of time for the shots of the boat, okay?"

"Looking forward to it," said Wildcat, dumping her script in Zak's lap and following Marnie down the beach. "See you," she called to Zak. Then she turned and aimed two fingers at his face, before pointing them all along the beach.

He nodded. He knew what that gesture meant. Keep your eyes peeled.

There was only one small problem with that suggestion. They hadn't seen Elton Dean all morning. It was hard to keep close tabs on someone who wasn't around.

There was nothing particularly suspicious about Dean being missing from the shoot. Half the time he was off somewhere else, making deals and fixing problems, but it was frustrating to have lost track of him so soon after the discovery of that note and the incident with the koi carp pond.

Zak flipped to the final few pages of the script, reading again the part where super-boy Tyler McFadden stops the bomb in the pumping station from causing a disaster. Zak had to smile. Tyler saves the day by throwing himself on the bomb and absorbing the explosion with his new super-tough body.

Zak imagined showing Dr Jackson back at Fortress how he was able to do the same. It was Dr Jackson who had first suggested that his ability to run fast was maybe just the tip of the iceberg as far as his physical powers might be concerned. He hadn't been wrong. Twice now, Zak had experienced a rush of energy that had given him extraordinary strength. The downside of it had been that he'd pretty much flaked out afterwards both times. The power might be there, but he couldn't summon it at will. And he certainly didn't plan on testing the super-toughness of his skin any time soon. He'd leave that to movie characters.

He looked up from the script. Cat was with the other two scantily clad and suntanned female extras, getting some final instructions from Grayson Clarke. As Zak watched, Wildcat shed her tracksuit and, dressed only in a black bikini, clambered into the boat.

"Looking a bit pale, there, Cat," murmured Zak. "Still, I expect they'll fix it in post-production. Give you a nice Californian suntan."

A couple of people pushed the boat out into deeper water. Wildcat started the motor and the boat moved away from the beach. Zak waved but she didn't notice.

What was it that Grayson Clarke always said?

"Roll sound. Roll cameras. Mark it. And . . . *action*!"

CHAPTER **SIX**

Zak was on the veranda outside the beachfront restaurant. He'd been told he wasn't needed until the afternoon. That was typical of this whole movie shoot, he thought. You're dragged out of bed first thing in the morning, rushed to a location and then told to wait around for six hours while they're busy with other things.

What was even more annoying was the fact that Elton Dean hadn't turned up today. It felt to Zak like a total waste of time to be sitting around here when the whole point of this mission was to keep a close eye on Dean. The rumour was that the producer was in negotiations with the local authorities in Benedict Canyon to get permission to mount a re-shoot of the out-of-control-bus sequence.

Zak wasn't sure how much he was looking forward to that. So far the police had no leads. The story had slipped from top spot in the prime-time news already. The TV crews had moved onto other things. Zak's fifteen minutes of fame were over. Or so he hoped.

Assistant Director Reed had told them that the FBI was on the case, but they had to keep their investigation at arm's length. The last thing they needed was for Elton Dean or one of Raging Moon's people to figure out the FBI were breathing down their necks. If they got spooked, they might close down the whole operation and set it up again somewhere else. And that would mean months of research coming to nothing.

"These guys have global reach," AD Reed had said. "If they quit California, and we lose track of them, they could set up shop anywhere on the planet. Europe, Africa, Asia. You name it. I'm sick of playing catch-up with these people. I want to nail them and I want to nail them right here, right now."

Zak stared out across the beach. The ocean sparkled in the dazzling sunlight and the motor boat was just a dark fleck out beyond the rolling breakers. There were two other boats alongside, loaded with cameras and movie technicians. Grayson Clarke was controlling the whole thing from the beach, sitting with a couple of other people under a canvas canopy and watching the action on monitor screens.

The way the light danced on the water made it hard to see anything clearly. Zak decided it was time to try out one of the Project 17 devices he'd brought with him. He took a case from his pocket. Inside was a pair of sunglasses. He put them on and looked out to sea again. That was much better – the glare was gone.

But the sunglasses did so much more. He pressed a finger to the right-hand side of the glasses. The image zoomed in at dizzying speed. Cat's boat had been no bigger than his fingernail a moment ago; now it almost filled his vision. He could see her and the two other girls sitting in the boat, waiting for the director to call for action. The scene involved the engine blowing up and the boat capsizing. There were frogmen out there, hidden from view, ready to tip the boat the moment the explosion went off.

Of course, there would be no real explosion, just a flash of light and smoke and a spray of harmless styrofoam debris thrown out of a special effects device called an air cannon.

He zoomed in a fraction more. Cat had her hand to the side of her head. She was talking to someone on a concealed headset. Zak guessed she was being given some last-second instructions from Grayson Clarke. Cat nodded, waved towards the beach and took off her headset.

Roll sound. Roll cameras. Mark it. And . . . action!

There was a long pause, then Zak saw the flash of light from the engine. The plastic shrapnel sprayed out and the boat tipped. The three girls staggered about and fell into the water. They splashed around while the cameras filmed them. Then the action stopped, the camera boats moved in and the girls were hauled out of the water.

Zak assumed that was it, but then he realized they were setting up to shoot the whole thing over again.

He remembered something he'd heard one of the crew saying. Grayson likes to shoot each scene up to twenty-five times, then he'll pick the best. He's such a perfectionist.

Cat might be in and out of that boat a couple of dozen times before they were through. She'd just love that!

The part where Tyler McFadden saves the girls was going to be filmed in a studio water tank with real actors at another time. The different sequences would all be edited together to make one smooth, seamless rescue scene.

Zak gazed out over the open ocean. He could see a few big ships on the horizon – even with his zoom-lens glasses, they were still no more than grey blurs.

Then he saw something that caught his interest. It was a very large yacht, shining white, with smooth, sleek lines, cruising along several hundred metres beyond the small cluster of movie boats. But the thing that really struck Zak was the helicopter sitting on a pad towards the stern of the yacht.

How expensive does a yacht need to be to have its own helicopter? Pretty expensive, he thought.

What puzzled him, though, was that he was sure he'd seen the yacht somewhere before.

He touched the side of his sunglasses to bring the zoom up to maximum. There were some people on the deck, sitting together, chatting and drinking.

Zak spotted another figure. A man, slightly apart from the others, leaning over the rail. Zak was almost certain it was Elton Dean. But doing what? Being seasick? Zak saw one of the men beckon to him. Elton Dean turned away from the rail, wiped his arm across his face, and walked back to join the others.

Weird. Elton Dean was supposed to be meeting with officials from Benedict Canyon. What was he doing out there? Had the story of the meeting been invented to mask Dean's real plans? If so, why? Zak frowned, suspicious now. And what was it about that yacht that made his secret agent senses tingle?

He did a quick mental trawl through the FBI folder on Elton Dean that they'd been shown in Washington. The guy owned a yacht, but it was nothing like as huge as this one. Half the size. This was not his yacht then. So, whose was it?

"How annoying must that be?" Zak murmured to himself. "Being invited on a luxury yacht and spending your time throwing up over the side?"

Then he saw something that made him sit up and stare.

There was a design on the super-structure, just in front of the helipad. Something circular. Zak leaned forwards, his finger tapping the side of the sunglasses to make absolutely sure they were on ultimate zoom.

For a moment, he'd thought the circular design was the same one he'd seen on the warning note – the snake eating its tail. But now he looked closer, he saw that it was a black and white representation of the Earth. He could see America and South America quite clearly on the left-hand side, with part of Africa and Europe to the right.

Zak reached for his Mob, meaning to call AD Reed or Colonel Hunter to tell them about the yacht and ask them to research that logo. But he hesitated. He'd been told not to use his Mob to make contact. It was safe from any known method of hacking, but on a mission like this, no chances could be taken. The only totally secure way of reaching AD Reed or Fortress was to use Wildcat's laptop – and that was back in Elton Dean's mansion.

He decided to wait.

A few more hours wasn't going to make much difference. Stay cool, and keep watching. He'd fill Cat in on what he'd seen as soon as they had the chance to be alone together.

Zak lifted his left hand and pressed a finger against the side of the sunglasses. He heard a faint series of clicks. Photos were being taken of the yacht. Photos that could be downloaded onto the laptop.

He turned his gaze to the stern again and took a series of pictures of Elton Dean and the other guys.

He had a feeling that he was finally on to something.

Zak had no chance to talk to Wildcat for some time after he'd seen the yacht. Grayson Clarke had insisted on twenty-three takes of the exploding boat set piece. By the time Cat and the other girls were finally allowed to come ashore, Zak had been whisked off to the props trailer to get into the look-a-like jeans and black leather jacket with the spread-winged golden eagle on the back that Tyler McFadden always wore.

Grayson Clarke gave him some final instructions. "Run down the beach as fast as you can, okay? Then dive in and swim for the boat. Plenty of energy, Zak. Lives are at stake, remember. Give it all you've got."

Zak did as he was told. Running on sand wasn't as easy as on a hard surface, and it took him a little while to really get into the zone – by which time he was almost in the surf. He loped into the shallow water then dived and started swimming. The honk of an air horn let him know when to stop. He swam back. People applauded as he walked up the beach.

"That was great, Zak," said Grayson Clarke. "Towel off and Marnie will dry your hair. Then we'll go for another take."

And another . . .

And another . . .

PACIFIC STANDARD TIME (LOS ANGELES): 22:15.
GREENWICH MEAN TIME (LONDON): 06:15.

Zak and Cat were back at the Parnassus Mansion at the end of a long, hard, exhausting day. Zak had lost track of how many times he'd run down the beach and dived into the water. Twenty, maybe? It felt more like twenty thousand. Running at top speed through the fine dry sand had been gruelling – and Grayson Clarke had kept asking him to go faster. By the end of the shoot, he'd felt like plunging into the Pacific Ocean, swimming for the horizon and never coming back.

But the two agents were finally alone and Wildcat's laptop was open for a conference call. Zak had wired the Project 17 sunglasses to a USB port, so Assistant Director Reed and Colonel Hunter could see the pictures he had taken of the yacht.

Now they were blown up on the screen, even more detail was visible. An interesting story emerged. The men sitting around on the sundeck of the yacht were smiling and drinking and seemed to be having a good time, but it was clear that Elton Dean was not enjoying himself. In fact, he looked nervous. Almost frightened. Zak was more convinced than ever that he'd seen Elton Dean throwing up over the back of the yacht. Not because he'd been seasick – because he was scared.

"That fits with some other information we've received," said Assistant Director Reed. "According to our sources, Dean has sent his sister and her entire family on an all-expenses paid trip to Hawaii. A very sudden trip. They dropped everything yesterday and just left."

"Is Mr Dean's sister Brandon Fine's mother?" asked Zak.

"She is," said AD Reed. "And Brandon has gone with her. What do you make of that?"

"He's getting his family out of harm's way," said Wildcat. "So they can't be targeted again."

"That's my take on it," said Assistant Director Reed. "Dean is scared, and Raging Moon is piling the pressure on to make sure he keeps to his side of the deal. Whatever's going down, my guess is it's going to happen soon."

"Agreed," said Colonel Hunter. "Did you notice? Something interesting happens in the final shots taken by Quicksilver. All the men seem to turn their heads at the same time."

Cat brought the pictures up on screen. Colonel Hunter was right – in the final two shots, everyone was looking in the same direction, as though someone had called to them from inside the boat. Their boss, maybe?

"It's a shame we don't get to see who it is," said Assistant Director Reed.

"But it's pretty obvious Dean isn't having a great time. What do you think, Peter? Is he getting his final instructions from Raging Moon? Could Raging Moon be on the boat?"

"It's possible," said Colonel Hunter. "Or if not actually aboard, certainly in contact with those who are. Take a look at the picture numbered P17013. It shows part of the yacht's name."

Cat flicked through the pictures. This one was focused towards the front of the yacht. Colonel Hunter was right. Cat tapped keys to zoom the picture in.

OURO

Ouro?

"The yacht has got to be called the *Ouroboros*," said Wildcat. "Bug told us that the snake eating its tail, the World Serpent, was sometimes called the Worm Ouroboros. So there must be some kind of link between that note Silver found and this yacht. It's too much of a coincidence otherwise."

"Oh, wow!" Zak gasped. He felt as if a light had just gone on in his head. "I know where I've seen that boat before. I don't believe it! This is way too spooky!"

"Explain," said the Colonel.

"Remember the mission in Montevisto?"

"Operation Tyrant King, yes," said Colonel Hunter.

"I'd swear this yacht was there," exclaimed Zak. He turned to Wildcat. "Do you remember it? When I went on board Alfonzo Gecko's yacht in the marina. It was moored at the far end of the jetty."

Wildcat's eyes narrowed. "I think you're right," she said. "I'd forgotten about it – but it was the same colour and it had a helipad for sure."

There was a curious silence from AS Reed and Colonel Hunter.

"There's no way this was a coincidence," insisted Zak. "And I remember where I know World Serpent from as well. Gabriel mentioned it – Agent Archangel, I mean. He asked me if I'd ever heard the name World Serpent, and when I said I hadn't he said that Colonel Hunter was playing it close to his chest . . . something like that . . ."

"Archangel was the MI5 man in Italy, wasn't he, Peter?" asked Assistant Director Reed. "I've seen the file. He and Zak brought down the criminal known as Padrone and helped flush out the mole in your organization."

"Correct," said Colonel Hunter.

It had been a weird mission. Truth be told, it hadn't been an authorized mission at all. Zak had gone off without telling anyone, chasing after information that had come from the man calling himself Gabriel. An MI5 deep-cover agent codenamed Archangel. Gabriel had told him there was a mole in British Intelligence – a mole so high up that even people like Colonel Hunter himself were under suspicion. The mole had turned out to be Colonel

Margaret Pearce of Citadel, chief of one of the four secret underground departments of MI5 in London.

One of the reasons Zak had been prepared to follow Gabriel was that he had once been a colleague of his brother, Jason. Zak had never known Jason – he'd been a three-month-old baby and Jason had been eight when their parents had been killed on a secret mission over Canada. Their aeroplane had been brought down. A Secret Service investigation concluded that an international terrorist who went by the name Reaperman had given the order that had killed them.

Long story short: Jason had been adopted, but Zak had wound up in a children's home. They had never met, and until a few months ago, Zak had not even known he had a brother – far less a brother who was an MI5 agent, an agent with the codename Slingshot. He had hoped that Gabriel might be able to tell him something about Jason, but in the end, there had been no time.

The only information Colonel Hunter had confided since then was that Agent Slingshot was working undercover – and that he was part of the international team trying to hunt down Reaperman. Zak could still remember exactly what the Colonel had said to him.

Don't go looking for your brother. When the time is right, the two of you will meet. You have my promise on that.

Zak snapped back into the present. "What does World Serpent mean, Control?" he asked. "You know, don't you?" He glanced at the two faces on the laptop's screen. Assistant Director Reed had her arms steepled together and her fingers to her lips, as though waiting. Colonel Hunter looked troubled.

"I'm not in a position to give you any information on that," he said at last.

"But Silver is right, isn't he?" said Wildcat. "You do know." Her eyes flicked from one to the other. "Both of you do. That's what you wanted to talk about in private yesterday. Why are you keeping us out of the loop on this? What does World Serpent mean?"

"All information is given on a need-to-know basis," the Colonel said guardedly. "You know that. Meanwhile, I don't want you speculating about it. That's an order. You are not to use those words, either in public, or when you believe no one can hear you. Is that understood?"

"Yes, Control," said Wildcat.

"Of course," added Zak, surprised by the hard edge to Colonel Hunter's voice.

"I'll put a team on finding out who owns the *Ouroboros* and where it's been recently," said AD Reed. "A super-yacht like that shouldn't be hard to track."

"I'll have Bug do the same from here," said Colonel Hunter. "Right now, we need you to carry on doing your jobs, agents. That's all. Fortress out."

Colonel Hunter's face vanished from the screen.

"I'm catching the red-eye to Washington in two hours," Assistant Director Reed told them. "Important conference with the Attorney General at the White House. I'll be out of Los Angeles for at least twenty-four hours. Contact the FBI field office in Wilshire Boulevard if you need anything." She gave them a quick nod. "That was good work with the yacht, Zak," she said. "Honour is due." Then she was gone.

Zak and Cat looked at one another.

"What is it with World Serpent?" Zak asked. "Why won't they let us in on it?"

"Top secret, I guess," muttered Wildcat. "Control didn't specifically forbid us to search the internet though, did he?" She opened a search engine and typed **World Serpent** into the search box. She gave a burst of laughter, pointing to the results.

About 54,700,000 results (0.27 seconds)

Zak glanced at the first page. Nothing stood out.

He stretched and yawned. "Good luck checking through that lot," he said, getting up. "I'm off to bed. See you in the morning."

"I don't think you will," Wildcat reminded him. "You have that location shoot, and I have the day off. Don't make too much of a racket when they drag you out of bed at six in the morning. I'm going to sleep in."

"Oh, great," said Zak. "Way to be a spy-girl."

"I won't be skiving," said Wildcat. "With any luck, Bug will be able to tell us where the *Ouroboros* has docked recently. If it's anywhere close, I'll go and check it out."

Zak opened the door. "Honour is due," he said as he went out.

"Yes it is," said Wildcat with a brief smile. "It certainly is."

Elton Dean's office was in darkness. He was sitting at his desk, staring at nothing, biting his lips. He jumped at the sudden sound of the phone, although he'd been expecting it to ring.

He picked up and held the receiver to his ear without speaking.

"We'll deal with your little problem tomorrow at the shoot," a voice told him.

"What are you going to do?" Had Wildcat been there to listen, she'd have recognized the same fear in his voice that she'd heard on the night of the party.

There was a good reason for that. He was talking to the same dangerous person. A person who filled him with dread.

"You'll find out soon enough," said the voice. "Trust me, after tomorrow, you won't have to worry about the boy ever again."

CHAPTER **SEVEN**

The sun was low in a clear blue sky as the convoy of movie trucks and cars made its way along Hollywood Boulevard and turned north into Beechwood Drive. The road was lined with tall, shaggy palm trees, and up ahead the Hollywood sign blazed out in huge white letters halfway up the green flank of Mount Lee.

Zak was in a car with Marnie, Grayson Clarke's assistant. She was full of information. "The sign is four hundred and fifty feet long, and the letters are forty-five feet high," she told him enthusiastically. She always sounded super-enthusiastic. Zak had the feeling her employment contract insisted on it.

He did a quick calculation in his head. That made the sign about one hundred and thirty-seven metres long and fourteen metres high. Impressive.

"It was originally put up in 1923," Marnie continued. "And it read 'Hollywoodland', but the last four letters were taken down."

Zak made an *uh huh?* noise, but he was only half-listening. He had other things on his mind. This time Elton Dean had come on the shoot. Zak was hoping that he'd spot something or overhear something that would give an idea of exactly what the millionaire producer had been strong-armed into doing.

If their guesses were correct, and Elton Dean had been on the yacht getting his final orders, the terrorist atrocity could happen any day now. But they still didn't know what it would be or where it was planned to happen. Unless they could find out more – and soon – their whole mission to Los Angeles would be a failure. And Zak was determined not to let that happen.

"Why are we driving away from the sign?" Zak asked, glancing over his shoulder as the huge white letters slid away behind the movie convoy.

"The real sign has been fenced in," Marnie explained. "And they have a high-tech security system to keep people out. It's really hard to get permission to shoot there these days."

"Especially if you want to blow it up," added Zak.

"We're heading northwest into the hills," said Marnie. "We're going to a place where we've built our own sign."

Zak gazed at her. "You built your own Hollywood sign?" he said.

Marnie nodded smugly. "We sure did."

"Wow," said Zak.

By the time Wildcat got up, Zak had already gone and the sun was over the mountains, blazing through the blinds at her bedroom window. She showered quickly, threw on some clothes and opened her laptop.

There was an email from Bug.

Vid me when you get this.

She opened the vid-link. Bug was sitting in his leather armchair in his usual position, feet up on his workstation, keyboard in his lap. Behind him she could see some of his collection of toy frogs gathered thickly on shelves. Bug had a thing for frogs.

The moment the link opened he began talking, without

taking time to say hello. Bug was better with computers than he was with people. "The *Ouroboros* was custom-built for a Russian billionaire named Vladimir Karpov a few years back," Bug told her. "But he sold it to a Greek TV company for one hundred million dollars two years ago." He was typing as he spoke. "That's when things get interesting. The Greek company was bought by an American-based international media corporation with a head office in New York, and branch offices in Chicago, Los Angeles, London, Hong Kong, Tokyo . . . etcetera."

"All over the world then?" said Wildcat.

"Pretty much," said Bug. "The company is called Worldwide Synergy."

Wildcat sat up sharply. "Worldwide Synergy owns the *Ouroboros*?" she exclaimed. Worldwide Synergy was the company that Bree Van Hausen worked for, she remembered. The crazy public relations woman Silver had met at the party was the Chief Executive Officer of the Los Angeles branch.

"As of last July they have," said Bug. "And in that time, the *Ouroboros* has certainly got around. I don't have data on all its movements, but I think Quicksilver was right about seeing the yacht in Montevisto – it was definitely in the northwest Mediterranean around the time you and Switch and Silver were there. And for the past two weeks, it's been berthed at the Mendocino Holiday Harbour in Wilmington, Los Angeles."

Wildcat typed quickly and a sub-screen opened, showing a satellite image of the port area of Los Angeles. It was a heavily built-up zone with lots of sharp-angled inlets and docking areas along the waterfront. "I can get there," she said. "Do you know where the yacht is right now?"

"Live satellite feed shows it in the dock," said Bug. "Control asked me to patch you through to him when we were done."

Again, no goodbyes. The screen simply changed to show Colonel Hunter.

"Has Bug filled you in?" he asked.

"Yes, sir. Are Worldwide Synergy suspected of being involved in the terrorist threat?"

"On the surface, the company seems to be entirely legitimate," said the Colonel. "But let's say they're on our radar now. At the moment, we have no evidence to suggest that Elton Dean's appearance on the yacht was anything other than a normal business meeting. Worldwide Synergy has been hired as public relations representative for the film *Adrenaline Rush*. It wouldn't be unusual for the producer to meet with the team running their PR campaign."

"But if it's all above board, it's kind of strange that the *Ouroboros* was in Montevisto the same time we were," said Wildcat.

"I agree," said the Colonel. "Which is why I need you to find out everything you can about the yacht. And I need Quicksilver to take up Bree Van Hausen's offer of going to her office for an interview. If Worldwide Synergy is being used as a front for a terrorist organization, she may not know anything about it. A legitimate international business concern run by people who know nothing of their true intentions may be the perfect cover for them. On the other hand, she could be involved in Raging Moon's plans. Either way, we need all the information we can get – and we need it fast."

"I'm on it, Control," said Wildcat. "I've got the business card Bree Van Hausen gave to Quicksilver. I'll call her office and arrange for him to go and see her as soon as he gets back from today's shoot." Wildcat was already rummaging through her bag for the blood-red calling card with the fancy white writing. Silver had given it to her for safekeeping. "And as soon as I've set that up, I'll get over to Wilmington and check the yacht out myself."

"Where's the rest of it?" Zak asked as he gazed up at the

fourteen-metre-high white letters **HOL** that stood on a long green hillside above where the movie convoy had come to a halt.

"We'll fill them in with CGI," said Grayson Clarke. "We only need the first three letters for the live action."

Zak gazed up the hillside. People were swarming around the three big white letters. "Are you actually going to blow them up for real?" he asked. "Or is that going to be CGI as well?"

"No, we'll be doing it for real," said Grayson Clarke. "Whenever we can go with real live action, we do, Zak. That's why you're here."

"But if you can't do it for real, you're okay with CGI?" asked Zak.

"You got it, Zak," said Grayson Clarke. "It's all part of the magic of movie-making." He pointed to the huge white letters. "Our top explosives experts have been here since dawn, setting up charges and squibs. It'll be spectacular, I can promise you that."

"I read in the script that I get chased by a helicopter," said Zak. "Is that going to be a real helicopter?"

"As real as it gets, Zak," said Grayson Clarke. "But don't worry, the stunt pilots know what they're doing. You won't come to any harm. Now, I need you in make-up, Zak. We'll be a while yet getting everything sorted, but I want you ready to go the moment I give you the mark."

Zak headed for the make-up trailer. He saw Elton Dean standing by a car, talking on his mobile. He looked ill, Zak thought. Ill or worried sick, perhaps?

"Thanks, I can find it from here," Wildcat paid the taxi driver and watched as the yellow cab glided away. She had been dropped off outside a gated area of white buildings and waving palm trees. A sign curved over the gates.

Welcome to the Mendocino Holiday Harbor

A smaller sign was fixed to one of the brick gateposts.

Access to tenants and authorized personnel only. Visitors to the harbor should use the intercom and await instructions

Okay, Wildcat thought as she peered through the tall iron rails, noting the CCTV cameras set up on almost every building. Tricky to slip in unannounced, and even trickier to move about without drawing attention, she imagined.

Was it time to play the dumb-blonde card? She really

hated doing that. But maybe she could give it a twist so it wasn't so bad?

She pressed the intercom button.

A male voice came from the grille. "How may I help you?"

"I've been sent here by Mr Dean of Parnassus Studios," said Cat, doing her best to mimic the breathless excitement that all of Elton Dean's assistants had. "I have some documents I need to hand over to Mr Dean's business associates on the *Ouroboros*." She patted her jacket pocket for the benefit of the CCTV cameras. "Thing is," she continued, "I forgot to bring Mr Dean's harbour pass, and the documents need to be signed, like, right now. Is there any way you can let me in without the pass?"

There was a moment's silence, then the lock on the wrought iron gate clicked.

"That's just fine, miss," said the voice. "You go on in."

"Oh, thank you so much," said Cat, slipping in through the gate. "You're a real lifesaver."

"Just doing my job, miss."

Wildcat saw the guard behind a window in a white building. She smiled and gave him a friendly wave. He waved back.

Amazing how well the damsel-in-distress act could work.

Cat walked through rows of recreational buildings, heading for the marina. There were plenty of people around, but no one took any particular notice of her. It was basic Project 17 tactics. Keep your head up, and make eye contact when appropriate. Don't deliberately avoid looking at people. Move briskly but don't seem to be in a hurry. Give the impression that you know where you're going. Confidence carries the day.

She crossed some well-tended grass and came out between two glass and steel buildings to find herself gazing at a vast network of slipways crowded with dozens of yachts.

Under normal circumstances, finding one particular yacht in such a huge marina might have taken a while, but the *Ouroboros* wasn't just any luxury yacht. Even among the wealthiest people in Los Angeles, it was special.

There it was – a few hundred metres away, towering over all the boats that surrounded it. There were plenty of people aboard, she noticed – in fact, there seemed to be some kind of party going on. A couple of trucks were drawn up close to the gangplank. Cat noticed the logo on the trucks.

LUX-TUX CATERING CO.

Interesting. They'd hired caterers. This was going to

be easier than she'd expected – she should be able to get on board and nose around without anyone noticing. A steady stream of men and women in white shirts and black waistcoats and red bow ties were coming and going up the gangplank, carrying trays of food and drink. Music sounded from the deck. Music and laughter and the crackle of conversation.

Wildcat scanned the people milling around the trucks, picking up food and drink. She homed in on a man with a clipboard who was shouting instructions.

"Excuse me," she said. "I'm really sorry I'm late. My car wouldn't start."

The man looked her up and down. "Who are you?"

"The agency sent me," Cat explained. "They said you needed some extra pairs of hands?"

"Where's your uniform?" the man snapped.

"No one told me it was formal," said Cat. "I'm so sorry."

"Never mind. There are some spare shirts and waistcoats in there." He pointed her towards the back of one of the trucks. "Find yourself something that fits and then get to work." He looked down at his clipboard. "We need more artichoke and tomato bruschetta," he called. "And who's in charge of the shrimp and andouillette sausage kebabs?" He marched off, leaving Wildcat to climb into the back of the truck and pick a uniform from a rack.

Five minutes later, she was walking along the gangplank with a tray of canapés balanced on her hand.

She smiled to herself. *And that, my friends, is what we in the trade call low-key infiltration.*

Now, all she hoped was that she'd learn something useful.

CHAPTER **EIGHT**

Zak was in the make-up trailer, sitting and staring at himself in a large brightly lit mirror while a woman called Jay worked on him. There were snapshots of Scott Blaine tacked up around the mirror, showing him in various different poses. Jay's task that morning was to style Zak's hair so it looked more like Scott's.

"That is such a cute accent you have, Zak," she said as she fussed over the way a single curl looped over his forehead. "You and your sister, both. I've always wanted to visit England . . . it's so exotic."

Zak looked at her in the mirror. England? Exotic? *Whatever.*

He and Wildcat were well-rehearsed in a full backstory

for Zak and Olivia Morrison. The two Morrison kids came from a happy home in Surrey, where their father worked as a technician in an electronics company and their mother ran a restaurant. They had been fed plenty of details and incidents that they could use if they were asked.

A bouncing melody sounded from Zak's Mob.

He fished it out of his jeans pocket. It was Switch's ringtone. A text.

Not work, surely? Switchblade was too experienced an agent to use the Mob for official business when they'd all been told they might not be secure.

Don't forget to take plenty of pictures while you're out there being a movie star. S.

P.S. Granddad H sends love.

Zak smiled, imagining how Colonel Hunter would react to being called 'Granddad'.

"That was a friend," Zak said to Jay. "From back home." He texted back.

Will do. How jealous are you on a scale of 1 to 10?

He put the phone down on the table, waiting for one of

Switch's trademark comebacks.

The door to the trailer swung open. "Zak's wanted on set, now," came a voice.

Jay pulled the make-up cape from around his shoulders as Zak got up. "Go get, 'em, tiger," she said. "You'll be great."

Wildcat glided among the partygoers, smiling and offering them canapés from her tray. She was listening carefully but all she caught was the same kind of trivial chatter she'd overheard at the big bash at the Parnassus Mansion.

She went back to the caterers' truck to replenish her tray then headed into the party again. She had images in her head of that bunch of guys who had been photographed by Quicksilver yesterday. They were the ones to look out for.

Then she saw one of them. She was certain it was him – a big man with buzz-cut silvery hair and a full-lipped, cruel sort of face. He was carrying a tray of drinks. Shot glasses. Scotch on the rocks. She moved closer to him as he made his way across the sundeck and went inside.

She followed. There were plenty of people gathered in the long, luxurious salon. The man cut through them and exited via another internal door. Trying to look as casual as possible, Wildcat offered canapés and smiled as she tracked him.

One of the great things about being a waitress at a function like this was that no one paid you any attention unless you were pushing a tray under their noses. Wildcat stood at the door. Making sure no one was looking, she slid out of the room.

The man was at the far end of a corridor. She paused until he moved out of sight, then she pattered after him.

She had contingency plans. *"What are you doing here?"*

"I'm so sorry, I got totally lost. This boat is huge! Can I interest you in an artichoke and tomato bruschetta?"

Damsel-in-distress act, scene two.

She tracked the man down a flight of stairs and along another corridor, heading deeper into the massive yacht.

He went into a cabin and closed the door behind him. Wildcat slid along the wall and pressed her ear to the door, every muscle in her body tense and poised to get out of there if the door opened or someone came along the corridor.

"Thanks, Carl," she heard someone say. "Sixteen-year-old malt whisky is just the thing for a toast like this!"

She heard other voices murmuring agreement.

The voice spoke again. "Raise your glasses, my friends. We are about to embark on our most significant venture yet!"

Wildcat jammed her head against the door. So far, this could be a bunch of Hollywood movers and shakers congratulating themselves on some movie deal. She needed to hear more.

"Here's to sweet Los Angeles water," said the voice. "With our very own special additive!" There was the chink of glasses and laughter and some cheering.

Weird kind of toast, Wildcat thought. *They're not drinking water. They're drinking scotch.*

"And Perry here tells me that the problem with the Brit kid has finally been solved," continued the voice.

Wildcat's heart jumped. The Brit kid? Quicksilver.

"Does British Intelligence think we're so dumb they can send a kid over here to spy on us without anyone noticing?" asked the voice. "We started running checks on him the moment that clown Dean told the boss about the boy acting suspiciously. Some undercover agent! It took us two days to find the truth about him." There was more laughter.

Wildcat bared her teeth in a grimace of anger and frustration. She had always prided herself on her professionalism, on her ability to go under the radar, and she knew Silver felt the same. But these guys had flushed them out in under forty-eight hours. That was really maddening, and potentially very dangerous.

"What about the girl pretending to be his sister?" someone asked.

The hair prickled on Wildcat's neck.

"She's one of them," said the main man. "But my guess is she's just window dressing. We can deal with her later. The boss says it's the boy who needs taking down – and taking down quick and hard." Wildcat's heart was in her mouth now. Their cover had been blown.

"What's the plan, Perry?" asked a different voice. "Come on, let us in on it."

"Well, let's say this," said yet another voice. "When that zippy Brit kid runs up the hill on the location shoot today, he'd better be running for his life!" There was a pause for laugher. "Because, let me tell you guys, that machine gun isn't going to be firing blanks!"

Zak paid close attention as Mitch Miller explained what he was meant to do. Mitch was the special effects coordinator for the movie, a grey-haired man with a neat grey beard and purple sunglasses that he never took off.

"Okay, Zak, we've marked out your path up the hill

with green dye," he said, one hand on Zak's shoulder as his finger indicated a zigzag course towards the three big letters. "We've planted squibs along both sides of the run. These will be set off in sequence, so it looks as if the guy in the helicopter is tracking you with his machine gun. He'll be using a mock-up of the M60E3 – a belt-fed machine gun that fires two hundred rounds per minute. The squibs won't be too noisy. There'll just be a bang and a flash of light and a kick of smoke, as though a large calibre bullet has gone into the hillside."

Zak nodded. This sounded exciting. But he hadn't forgotten the reason he and Wildcat were here. To stop a terrorist attack. He wondered briefly how Cat was doing – whether she'd managed to get aboard the *Ouroboros*. He wished he could be doing something to help. However much fun he was having, it was annoying the way the movie got in the way of their real mission in Los Angeles.

The helicopter had arrived a few minutes ago, black and sinister-looking with two stunt men aboard. It had disappeared over the hill and gone quiet, waiting for its cue.

"As you'll know from the script, the guy in the chopper gives up on his automatic and grabs a bazooka to fire at you." Mitch slapped Zak on the back. "Don't sweat it,

Zak – it won't be real. Here's how it works. We're going to set off a fire cannon, okay? It'll give out some heat and smoke and it'll shoot some debris into the air. Things will be pretty intense for a few seconds, then it'll be over. The debris won't come near you. When I'm about to set off the fire cannon, I'll call 'fire in the hold'. When you hear that, you drop to the ground and stay down till you get the word that it's safe. Got that?"

"Got it," said Zak.

He walked over to where Grayson Clarke had set up his monitors. Elton Dean was there as well, looking sweaty and uncomfortable.

"Elton, calm down," he heard Grayson Clarke saying as he approached. "Nothing's going to go wrong today. I've worked with these guys plenty of times before. They're experts. The explosives have been checked and double-checked. The whole rig has been taken apart and put back together by people I trust completely. It will be fine."

So, Elton Dean was freaking out. Zak wasn't sure what to make of that. Did he think Raging Moon was going to give him another of those deadly warnings? Or was Elton Dean climbing the walls because he knew something bad was going to happen soon – not here, but somewhere else?

"Ready for your scene?" Grayson Clarke asked Zak.

"I can't wait," said Zak, watching Elton Dean. The man was perspiring freely, and after a quick glance at Zak, he turned and walked away.

"Okay, everyone, we're ready to go," Grayson Clarke said into a microphone. "Is the helicopter ready?"

"Waiting for the word," came an electronic voice.

Grayson Clarke smiled at Zak. "Plenty of energy," he said. "Your life is at stake – you have to get behind those letters or you'll be killed. We need to try and nail this in one take, Zak, otherwise we'll have to set all the pyro effects again – and that costs time and money."

One take? Excellent. It was quite a steep hill and Zak hadn't been looking forward to running up it over and over all day.

"Pyros hot," Grayson called. Mitch Miller raised a thumb as he flipped the red switch on his effects control board. "Chopper to start position." There was a sound of rotor blades beating the air as the black helicopter came into view above the hill behind the letters.

Zak shielded his eyes from the sun as he watched the helicopter curve around and hover high above them. The gunman stood in the open doorway of the fuselage, waving to show he was ready. He had the machine gun slung over his shoulder. Zak assumed the bazooka was out of sight inside the helicopter.

Zak stood at the foot of the hill, bouncing on his toes, shaking his arms and rolling his shoulders, sucking in big lungfuls of air and blowing it out again. He stared fixedly up the hill, following the marked-out contours of his run, focusing on what he was about to do. Getting his mind into the zone.

"Everyone ready?" called Grayson Clarke above the roar of the helicopter. "Roll sound. Roll cameras. Mark it. And . . . *action*!"

Zak sprinted forwards, concentrating on the ground three steps ahead. Scrutinizing the terrain, alert for any obstacles or problems. His arms pumped at his sides, his toes digging in, the muscles in his legs contracting and releasing in a swift, steady rhythm.

He was in the zone in moments. Flying, jinking this way and that as he followed the green spray-marker. He glanced up. The huge white letters loomed above him. He could hear the helicopter's engine and the throb of the rotor blades as it swooped in behind him.

Then there was the crackle of machine-gun fire and the whine of bullets. Smoke rose as the special-effects squibs tore through the hillside at his heels.

Zak raced on, speeding along effortlessly. He was having the time of his life.

CHAPTER **NINE**

Wildcat waved for a passing cab as she ran down South Pacific Avenue. The yellow taxi cruised to a halt and she threw herself onto the back seat, giving the driver breathless instructions. "And step on it!" she finished. "I have to be there *now*!"

With a screech of tyres, the cab was off. Wildcat pressed Quicksilver's number on speed dial on her Mob.

She'd already tried him twice with no response.

Third time lucky.

The moment she'd heard the guy behind the closed door talking about live ammunition, she'd known Silver was in mortal danger. She'd run, taking out her Mob as she went. Forget security concerns for the moment. He had to be warned – and quickly.

She had caused some commotion as she'd barged her way through the party people on the yacht and sprinted down the gangplank, wishing she had Quicksilver's speed.

She hadn't even paused at the gates of the harbour. She'd gone straight over them, using all her athletic ability to climb up and drop down safely on the far side – leaving the security guard shouting in her wake.

She held the Mob to her ear as the cab sped along. "Come on, come on!" she gasped. "Answer the phone!"

Something hot whizzed past Zak's face, making him flinch and stumble for a moment. A stuttering line of smoke and earth spurted ahead of him.

Realistic special effects or what?

He became aware of people shouting from below. He glanced over his shoulder. It was chaotic down there. People were gesticulating and yelling; others were staring dumbstruck up at the hovering helicopter.

Something was wrong. Mitch Miller had moved away from the special-effects control console and was waving his arms frantically.

Zak looked up. Fingers of flame were shooting out of the muzzle of the machine gun.

Not special effects.

Real bullets.

Live ammo – two hundred rounds a minute.

Zak suppressed a burst of panic. Scattered thoughts cartwheeled through his brain. His cover had been blown. Raging Moon had seen through his cover. He'd failed the mission. He'd let the Colonel down. And Wildcat? Was she in danger too? Was she already dead?

Zak's survival instincts and training kicked in – abilities and skills honed to perfection by hours of hard physical training.

He darted aside as machine-gun fire sprayed the hillside directly ahead of him, throwing up jets of dirt as the bullets smacked into the ground. Again he changed direction, speeding across the hill, running faster than he had ever run in his life.

He was so deep in the zone by now that he was hardly aware of physical effort as he sped to and fro up the steep face of the hill. He had no thought in his head other than to keep avoiding the spitting bullets, to get up to the big white letters and use them for cover.

As the hill grew steeper, Zak used his hands and feet to propel him forwards. The letters were getting closer, just a few metres away. His head was pounding from the noise of the helicopter as it closed in, the bullets tearing up the ground all around him.

Then he was there. He flung himself behind the hollow framework of the letter **L**, flattening his body to the ground as a stream of screaming bullets cut into the grass only centimetres away from him.

Now what?

His heart was crashing against his ribs. Not from effort – from fear. He might be safe for the moment, but the helicopter only needed to sweep around behind the letters and he'd be an easy target.

The snarl of the machine gun stopped suddenly. The throb of the spinning rotor blades sounded even louder now, even more menacing.

Zak crawled to the end of the letter and peered up.

The helicopter was hanging in the sky above him, turned sideways so he could see the open door in the fuselage. The gunman was gone.

Out of ammo?

Zak got warily to his feet, still keeping behind the long white leg of the huge letter. Was that it? Had they failed? Was it over?

He'd been too quick for them!

He'd outrun bullets. Wow!

The man reappeared in the doorway.

He had a bazooka over his shoulder.

There was no one in the make-up trailer. Jay, Zak's make-up artist, had gone with the others to watch the special effects.

Zak's Mob was sitting on the table.

There was a text from Switchblade, back in London.

Jealous of you in Hollywood? Please! When you've been round the world twice like I have, we'll talk about who's jealous of who!

There were also two missed calls from Wildcat.

As the bullets flew outside, the empty trailer echoed to the sound of Wildcat ringing again.

Her attempt to warn him had come too late. Way too late.

Zak had a fraction of a second to react as he saw a blast of red flame shoot out of the front of the bazooka. He hurled himself sideways, rolling as he landed.

A huge explosion rocked the hillside as the bazooka

shell punched through the plywood face of the letter. Zak's eyes were full of fierce red light and his ears rang with the noise. He was tossed through the grass by the shockwaves from the detonation. Debris rained down as black smoke billowed up.

He pulled himself to his hands and knees in time to see the towering letter **L** begin to topple. Flames were licking around the framework of wooden struts as the letter crashed down the hillside.

Shaking dirt out of his hair, Zak got to his feet, keeping out of sight behind the huge lower curve of the letter **O**. If they thought they'd killed him they might decide to get out of here before the cops showed up.

But he heard the beat of the rotor blades getting louder. The helicopter was moving closer. They wanted to make sure.

Zak pushed his hand into his pocket. His fingers closed around the small black rubber ball that he had been given by the white-coats in Fortress. One of his Project 17 gadgets. The black ball was officially known as a SGD706/E03, but everyone called it a whizzer.

He drew the whizzer out, watching the helicopter from his cover. The gunman was half-hidden inside. Zak guessed he was reloading, ready to fire again. He only had seconds to act.

Zak jumped onto the under-curve of the **O**. The pilot could see him now. The engine whined as the helicopter descended towards him.

Zak took the ball in both hands and gave it a sharp twist. The two sides moved against each other. He felt the click rather than heard it. He twisted it again, the other way now. Another click. A third twist and the whizzer was primed.

He had ten seconds.

The guy with the bazooka moved back to the open doorway. Zak spread his feet, stabilizing himself. He drew his arm back and flung the ball with all his strength. For a horrible moment, he thought his aim had been off. But the ball just scraped in at the bottom left hand corner of the doorway.

Three ... two ... one!

A cloud of dense white smoke erupted inside the helicopter, engulfing the bazooka-man. Poised to run if he had to, Zak watched as the smoke blotted out the face of the pilot and rolled across the windscreen. He heard the loud cracks and shrill, piercing whistling noises from inside the helicopter as the whizzer did its thing.

Blinding smoke. Deafening noise. All aimed at disorienting an enemy and gaining an advantage over them. And it was working.

The helicopter rose steeply, its engine shrieking. Zak could imagine the blinded pilot wrestling with the controls, desperate to avoid clipping the tops of one of the letters. He saw something fall from the open door. Long. Green. Metallic. The bazooka! It came crashing down and exploded in a plume of red and black smoke.

The helicopter rose higher, dark clouds pouring from it as it turned and sped away over the hilltop. Moments later, it had disappeared. Zak listened intently for the sound of a crash, but it never came. The pilot must have managed to keep control long enough for the smoke to blow away.

As the noise of the helicopter faded, Zak was once again aware of people shouting from the foot of the hill. A few were running and scrambling towards him, looking shocked and panicked. He waved to show he was okay.

All in a day's work.

Except that his heart was still pounding and he felt sick. There was no way that was another warning for Elton Dean. That had been up close and personal, and Zak had been the target.

Wildcat arrived at the location in the Santa Monica

mountains to find the area cordoned off by the police. She could see that something had happened. Flames were licking around the fallen letter **L** halfway up the hill. For a horrible few moments, she thought Quicksilver might be dead.

Then she saw him, sitting on the steps of a trailer, talking to a police officer. Elton Dean was also visible, sitting in the back of his limousine with the door open, looking ashen and sweaty.

More police officers were taking statements, and official photographers were videoing the scene.

It was time to act the anxious sister.

She ran towards Zak, pushing past people, calling out his name. "Zak! Are you okay?" She threw herself at him, sobbing. Her mouth came close to his ear. "The bad guys know who you are," she whispered, hugging him tightly. "They want rid of you. I'll fill you in when I can."

She drew away, looking into his eyes. "You must have been so frightened," she wailed. "What happened?"

"And you are?" asked the police officer Zak had been talking to.

"I'm his sister, Olivia," said Wildcat, adding a hysterical edge to her voice. "Tell me what *happened*!"

"Your brother is just fine," said the officer. "There

was an incident of live fire with a helicopter that was being used in the movie. The men who were supposed to be in the helicopter were found in the hanger back at Altadena, drugged and tied up. The helicopter was found abandoned a couple of miles from here. So far, we have no information as to the whereabouts of the two hijackers."

"You mean my brother was shot at?" gasped Wildcat.

"I'm fine, sis," said Zak. "They think this was done by the same people who sabotaged the bus and killed Chet Blake." His eyes widened – for the benefit of the police officer, Wildcat knew. "They think someone is out to wreck the whole movie!"

"And it looks as though they've succeeded – in the short term at least," said the officer. "The captain's closed down the movie until we can find out who's behind these attacks."

Zak heard the sound of a car approaching. He looked around in time to see a bright red Lexus Convertible screech to a halt. Bree Van Hausen stepped out and strode through the police cordon with a determined look stamped on her face.

She marched over to Elton Dean's car and leaned inside to speak to him. Zak saw him shaking his head and gesturing weakly at her. She stood up and turned to survey the scene.

"I want to speak with whoever is in charge," she called.

A police captain walked over to her.

"I'm told you think you can shut this movie down," she said to him, her eyes flashing. "I have just got off the phone with your commander. He agrees that the movie will carry on being made. We have legal obligations and deadlines, Captain. We can't afford to lose time – and time is money. More money per day than you'd earn in your entire lifetime. Do you get me?"

"I'm sorry, ma'am, but—"

Bree Van Hausen raised her hand and held it close to the police captain's face, stopping him short. "Call your boss, Captain, if you need to," she said dismissively. "But the shoot will go on. Just do your job and find out who is behind these atrocities." Her voice had an acid edge. "Do you think you can manage that, or should I ask Commander Burke to handle the case personally?"

The captain touched a finger to the side of his cap and turned away from her. Zak could see the controlled annoyance in his expression.

"Woah!" said the officer standing with Zak and Cat. "She's some piece of work.'

"Oh, indeed," muttered Wildcat.

Zak and Cat looked at one another. They needed to confer.

THE PARNASSUS MANSION, LOS ANGELES, CALIFORNIA.
PACIFIC STANDARD TIME (LOS ANGELES): 14:50.
GREENWICH MEAN TIME (LONDON): 22:50.

Zak and Cat were in Cat's room. The laptop was showing a local news channel. Once again, the *Adrenaline Rush* shoot was headline news. A TV helicopter was cruising over the mocked-up part of the Hollywood sign, showing the broken and burned out letter **L**. Breathless reporters were on-site, giving sound-bite accounts of what had happened. The police commander was on the steps outside his office, explaining how the police were throwing all their resources behind bringing the perpetrators of these crimes to justice.

Bree Van Hausen was also being interviewed, and she had an interesting take on what was going on.

"I am entirely convinced that this disruption is being caused by people who want the production of this amazing movie shut down. *Adrenaline Rush* is guaranteed to be a huge crowd-pleaser, and I'm sorry to say, there are some people in our beautiful city who simply can't stand the competition. They will not succeed. The shoot will go on as planned. Tomorrow is a big day. Grayson Clarke has been given permission to shoot at the Oakleaf Canyon Water Pumping Station. The whole *Adrenaline Rush* team will be there first thing in the morning as planned."

The interviewer stopped her. "Are you saying that these terrible acts have been committed by a rival movie company?"

"I'm not in a position yet to name names," Bree Van Hausen replied smoothly. "But I certainly have my suspicions. *Adrenaline Rush* is a prestigious, high-concept action movie that is guaranteed to have the biggest grossing opening weekend since . . ."

Cat turned the sound down. "Does she genuinely believe that?" she asked Zak. "Or it is just a cover?"

"I have no idea," said Zak. "It could be either, but she's a total headcase, that's for sure."

"Well, you'll have the chance to make your mind up about her this evening," said Cat. "I've arranged for you to meet at her offices at six-thirty."

They had already exchanged notes on the day's events so far.

Even if Worldwide Synergy wasn't involved with the terrorists, they were most definitely using the *Ouroboros* – the conversation Cat had overheard on the yacht proved that beyond any doubt. And the terrorists knew that Zak was a British spy. How? Was there a leak in the FBI? Had they done some digging and found out about Project 17?

Cat opened the vid-link to Fortress.

Colonel Hunter turned out to be fully informed of what had happened via his FBI contacts. And he had some bad news.

"I've heard from Assistant Director Reed in Washington," he told them. "The word is that Raging Moon's attack is planned to take place in the next twenty-four hours." His face was even more grim than usual. "Wildcat, I want you to do another sweep of Elton Dean's offices in the mansion – *find* something, agent! Take the risks I told you not to take. We're out of time."

"On it, Control," said Cat.

"Quicksilver," the Colonel barked. "Make that meeting with Bree Van Hausen count. Record everything she says and take plenty of pictures. Do you still have Bug's memory stick?"

"Yes, Control," said Zak. The USB stick with the password-finding Trojan Horse program on it was safe in his pocket.

"Find a way to access her computer," said the Colonel. "I don't care what methods you use. Do whatever it takes. Get into her computer and download everything you can. Bug will start working on it the moment you mail it to us from Wildcat's laptop. Don't worry about the time zone differences. Just get it done, even if it comes to us in the middle of the night."

"Got it, Control," said Zak.

"Now then," said the Colonel. "I don't have to tell you how vital this mission is, agents. Be smart. Be safe. Get the job done. Fortress out."

The screen went blank.

Zak and Cat looked at one another for a moment.

They had their orders.

Get the job done.

CHAPTER **TEN**

**WORLDWIDE SYNERGY LOS ANGELES
BUREAU.
FIFTEENTH FLOOR, SABLE TOWER, GRAND
AVENUE, LOS ANGELES.**

A limousine whisked Zak through the hectic, towering streets of the downtown business area of Los Angeles. He was wearing the look-a-like Tyler McFadden black leather jacket with the golden eagle on the back. It was top quality Italian leather – and he looked good in it. Part of him hoped he'd be allowed to keep it when the mission was over. But he had other things on his mind right now. He was trying to come up with a way of gaining access to Bree Van Hausen's computer without being caught. Not easy.

The car drew up in front of a large plaza. A black and silver tower shot up into the sky, the tinted glass windows reflecting the golden sunset. An area of the plaza was fenced off and Zak could see cement mixers and cranes and other signs that some major building work was in progress.

A young man in a dark suit was waiting for Zak as he got out of the car. "Welcome to Worldwide Synergy, Los Angeles Bureau," he said, smiling the usual California smile. "My name is Byron Venn; I'm Miss Van Hausen's personal assistant. She is so looking forward to meeting with you." Zak walked alongside as they headed across the plaza and into the tall building.

"Apologies for the disruption," Byron said, gesturing to the fenced-off zone. "They're in the middle of sinking the foundations for another tower. The work is going on twenty-four seven, I'm afraid. Very noisy and dirty, but what can you do?" He strode across a wide foyer towards a bank of silver lifts.

They stepped inside and he spoke into a grille on the wall. "Fifteenth floor, please."

"My pleasure," said a cool female voice and the lift

doors closed. Zak smiled to himself as they ascended. Talking lifts now? Only in America.

The lift came to a stop and the doors slid open. "Have a nice day," purred the lift as the door closed behind them. As Byron led him along, Zak was aware of red carpets and rooms with glass walls and stark modern furniture. Plenty of people were still at work, tapping away at computers or talking on telephones in their little cubicles.

Byron took him through a set of double doors into a suite of rooms that didn't have glass walls. Bree Van Hausen was waiting at the open doors to her private office.

"It is so great to meet you like this, Zak," she said, flicking Byron away with long red-nailed fingers and ushering Zak into her office. "I'll call if I need you again, Byron," she said as she shut the door. She turned to Zak again. "There now, we can have a little privacy. May I get you something, Zak? A drink? Soda? Ice water?"

"No, I'm fine thanks," Zak said. She gestured towards two low couches that faced one another across a black marble coffee table.

"Let's make ourselves comfortable," she said, guiding him to the couch then sitting opposite and crossing her long elegant legs.

Zak glanced around the room. There were awards and certificates on the walls. There was a desk with a computer on it. There was a picture window that looked out over the Los Angeles skyline, the high-rise tower blocks burning with thousands of lights as the sun went down.

His brain was buzzing. *How on earth am I going to get at her computer?*

He still had no idea.

"So, then, here we are," said Bree Van Hausen, smiling like someone had shoved a coat hanger in her mouth. "What shall we talk about first, Zak? How about that awesome running thing you can do? Would that be a good topic to break the ice?" The smile became even wider. "No, wait! I know. Let's talk about how such a young guy as you gets to work in a top-secret British Intelligence department like Project 17."

Back at the Parnassus Mansion, Wildcat was passing the time listening to a local news channel on her laptop while doing some exercises on the floor. She'd done one hundred each of push-ups and sit-ups and lunges, and she was halfway through some abdomen-tightening crunches when the croak of an American bullfrog rang through her room. She knew that particular call-sign.

She got up and threw herself across the bed to where the laptop was standing.

She pressed a key and Bug's face appeared. "What are you doing up, Bug? It must be the middle of the night over there."

"I couldn't sleep," said Bug. "I've been doing some research. I thought it might make me drowsy, but it's woken me right up. Control said I should contact you immediately. Has Quicksilver gone yet?"

"Yes, about an hour ago. Why?"

"I've done some more background on the *Ouroboros*," said Bug. "Remember I told you it was in the northwest Mediterranean at the same time that you and Switch and Silver were working Operation Tyrant King? Well, not too long after that the yacht was harboured for a brief time in the Autorità Portuale di Venezia."

Wildcat frowned, searching her memory. "That's in Venice," she said. Her eyes widened. "Don't tell me it was there at the same time that Switch and Silver were bringing down Padrone?"

"It was," Bug confirmed. "And what's more, it left port the morning after the fire in the office of Vice President Dante Rizzo in the Banca Mondo building in San Marco."

Quicksilver had set that fire, with the aid of Switchblade and a deep-cover MI5 agent known as

Archangel. Dante Rizzo had been the man running the mole in British Intelligence.

"Have you heard the phrase 'everything is connected'?" asked Bug. "I'm thinking that maybe the *Ouroboros* is the thread linking a lot of bad events together."

Wildcat nodded, her brain whirling. "It was there for Operation Tyrant King," she muttered. "Also for the rogue trip Quicksilver went on that got written up as Operation Talpa. And now it's *here*, right now."

"There's more," said Bug. "I did some back-door research on the yacht, and I came up with the documentation that signed it over to Worldwide Synergy. The name of the person who led the negotiations for the purchase was a woman named Rachel Morse."

Wildcat leaned towards the screen. "And . . . ?"

"Rachel Morse is an American citizen, born thirty-five years ago in the Brentwood district of western Los Angeles," Bug explained. "Except she isn't and she wasn't. It turns out Rachel Morse is an alias used by a very disturbing woman indeed. Here's a picture of her taken about fifteen years ago."

A grainy picture appeared on Wildcat's laptop. It was one of those high-angle CCTV stills – and it seemed to show a bank robbery in process. People were lying face down on the floor while three figures with machine guns stood over them.

"This was taken during a raid on a bank in Montevisto. The three people with the guns are members of the Montevisto Anti Royalist Strike-force."

"MARS!" gasped Wildcat. "The terrorist group that wanted the King of Montevisto dead."

"Exactly," said Bug. The picture zoomed in on one of the standing figures. They were all masked, but one mask had slipped to show a large portion of the person's face.

It was a young woman with short dark hair. Despite the gap of fifteen years, Wildcat had no trouble recognizing her. "It's Bree Van Hausen!"

"Kind of," said Bug. "She's also Rachel Morse, Brenda McMillan and Pauline DiMarco. Her real name is Aurore Marat. She was born in France to wealthy parents. Educated in America. Graduated from Yale with honours – at which point she seems to have gone completely mental. She met with some terrorists in New York in her early twenties and got recruited to their cause. She went to Europe and after about six months she was caught in the crackdown on MARS and sentenced to twenty-five years in jail. But she escaped from the van taking her to prison and was never heard from again. Right up until now."

"Bree Van Hausen is a known terrorist?" said Wildcat.

"We've just sent Silver to her office!"

"That's why Control asked me to contact you. At the moment, he's on the line with Assistant Director Reed, trying to reassess the situation now that we know exactly who's running the Los Angeles office of Worldwide Synergy."

"The terrorists want Silver dead, Bug!" exclaimed Wildcat, springing up off the bed. "I have to go and get him."

"Quicksilver can look after himself, Cat," said Bug. "Wait to hear from Control before you do anything crazy."

"Yeah, right!" Wildcat slammed the laptop closed and leaped for her wardrobe. She needed some clothes and she needed them quick.

Silver could be walking straight into a trap. She had to get over there.

Zak's brain was working at top speed as he sat staring at the smiling woman. How could she possibly know about Project 17? A department of British Security so secret that only a handful of top government officials had ever heard of it.

"Project *what* was it?" he asked, trying to gain time,

trying to pull a plan out of the hat. "I was never any good with numbers."

"Don't try to be cute with me," said Bree Van Hausen, her smile never slipping. "We know who you are, Agent Quicksilver, and we know who sent you and why you're here."

Zak leaned back, hands behind his head. Faking confidence. "If you already know it all, why ask?" he said, watching her carefully, wondering whether he could use his speed to get out of here before things got even more tricky.

"You're a little boy with a big job to do, aren't you?" she said. "You and your sweetie-pie girlfriend come six thousand miles to bring down the big bad Raging Moon."

"She's not my girlfriend," said Zak. "And if she heard you calling her a sweetie pie, she'd twist your head off and drop kick it into the Pacific." He forced his voice to remain calm. But he wasn't calm. His whole body was tensed like a coiled spring, waiting for the right moment to act. He'd been taught some martial-art moves that would take her down hard and fast.

But could he make his move on her without alerting Byron and the others out there? How much time would he have to search her computer before they came for him?

"She sounds like a bad girl," said Bree Van Hausen.

"No. She's good. You're the bad one – you and that nutjob boss of yours."

Her eyebrows rose. "What nutjob boss would that be?"

"Raging Moon."

She laughed. "You think Raging Moon is my *boss*?" she said. "I do like you with your sweet little accent and all – but you're kind of dumb, you know. Get with the curve, buddy. In a modern society women don't *have* bosses – women *are* the boss."

Wildcat had seen messengers coming and going from the Parnassus Mansion on motorbikes. She knew where the bikes were kept. She wanted one.

She opened the door of the garage and slipped inside. Flicking the light on, she walked along the rows of motorbikes.

"A Harley Davidson Seventy-Two, with a blockhead 1200cc electronic fuel-injected engine," she murmured, stroking the metallic red finish of the bike that had taken her eye. "You'll do."

Five minutes later, Cat was dressed in black leathers stolen from a locker in the garage, and she was riding the bike down to the gate. This wasn't a time to be subtle. Silver's life was at stake. She stopped at the gate and beckoned the guard over. No room for messing about. Get the job done.

In twenty-three seconds flat, the gate guard lay unconscious and Cat was steering the Harley Davidson Seventy-Two out onto the road. She was wearing a backpack. In the backpack was her laptop. She couldn't say for certain, but she had the feeling that their stay at the Parnassus Mansion was probably at an end.

She paused for a moment to bring down the visor on her full-face helmet, then she gunned the throttle, leaned into the wind and took off.

The revelations were coming almost faster than Zak could take them in. Bree Van Hausen was leaning back on the couch, smiling, in control of the situation and completely relaxed.

"You're Raging Moon?" Zak asked.

"I am," she said. She frowned. "Do you think the name's a little over the top? I liked it when I came up with it, but I'm not so sure now."

"You're responsible for Chet Blake's murder?"

"I am," she said. "That was a shame. He was a nice

guy. But Elton was getting squirrelly on me, you know. He needed to understand I meant business. Nothing says you're serious quite like death and mayhem. Know what I mean?"

Zak stared at her. She was crazy.

"All those kids in the bus could have been killed," he said.

"Most of them would probably have made it," she replied casually. "I expected the bus to hit something, turn on its side, skid a bit." She shrugged. "A few broken bones, bruises, cuts and grazes, maybe a snapped neck or two."

That did it. She was totally out of her mind.

"We know you've got something planned," Zak asked. "How exactly is Mr Dean involved? What is it you want him to do for you?"

She gave a laugh. "Do you think I'm going to sit here and explain the whole plot to you like some kind of cartoon villain?" She leaned forwards, and for the first time the smile was gone. "That's *not* how it works in the real world, buddy. Let me tell you what's actually going to happen."

"I can't wait." Zak held her gaze. There was something deeply scary about her, but he wasn't about to let on how much this situation was freaking him out.

"Oh, you've been trained well," she said, her eyes narrowing. "You're trying to figure out whether you have the guts to jump me. You've done it in the gym, but can you do it for real; that's the question going round and round in that tiny little head of yours."

"Actually, I was wondering what loony bin you escaped from," Zak said levelly. "And why they don't keep a closer watch on their patients." He leaned closer. "You see, the thing is . . ." He lunged forwards, throwing himself across the low table, snatching for her wrists as he cannoned into her.

The couch tipped backwards, but not before he saw a feral snarl twisting her face. He had hold of her wrists, and he was on top of her, pinning her down.

She let out a shout. He didn't have a hand free to gag her. And she was struggling hard now, kicking and writhing under him. He heard a door open. Feet running across the carpet. If he could just flip her and get her in some kind of choke hold, he'd have something to bargain with.

Something hit the back of his head and pain exploded in his skull. He toppled to one side, seeing flashes of red. He lay gasping. A foot pressed into his neck. He could hardly see for the agony that was pulsing behind his eyes. He was aware of Raging Moon scrambling to her feet.

He squirmed around and his vision cleared enough for him to see Byron Venn pointing a gun at him.

"Well, now," Raging Moon said breathlessly, straightening her clothes and smoothing her hair back into place. "That was very rude of you, but it seems you do have the guts after all." She crouched at his side. "I wasn't being entirely honest with you when I said I was the boss. I'm running the show here in California, but I do answer to someone else. And that person would love to meet you. I've spoken to him recently, and he doesn't want you dead after all. He wants you on a plane out of America." Her voice hissed with spite and venom. "He wants you in his laboratory so his people can do some research on you." Her fingers reached down and grabbed his face, the nails digging into his flesh. "They're going to find out what makes you able to run so fast. They're going to learn what makes you tick." She gave a manic grin. "Do you know what vivisection is, buddy-boy? Do you know what it feels like to be carved apart piece by piece while you're still alive and conscious? Well, my speedy little friend, you're going to find out."

She stood up. "Lock him up," she said. "We'll deal with him later. I have a TV interview in half an hour. *Adrenaline Rush* isn't going to promote itself." She looked at Zak. "Here's a clue for you. In twelve hours, about one and a half million people in Los Angeles are going to wish they had hydrophobia." She smiled. "It's going to be a big day tomorrow. A day no one is ever going to forget."

Zak stared up at her. He saw Byron's arm come hurtling down towards him. He saw the metallic gleam of the gun in his fist. He felt another blow to the side of his head.

This time the pain lasted only a couple of seconds.

CHAPTER **ELEVEN**

Zak woke up to a head full of deep, throbbing agony. The source of the pain was the spot where Byron's gun had struck him, but it radiated right through his skull, down his neck and into his body.

He groaned, turning over in the darkness. His vision was flecked with white and red. He felt sick.

He lay on the floor, trying to gather himself. Thin strips of light floated into vision, filtering in around a closed door. Slowly he began to make out his surroundings.

He was in a stationery cupboard. He sat up, wincing. But already the pain was fading. He'd noticed on previous occasions that pain never lasted long. Dr Jackson had told him it was probably a side effect of the adrenaline imbalance. Somehow it speeded recovery.

He got to his feet. His legs felt a little shaky. He went to the door and listened hard. Nothing. Not a sound. He felt in his pockets. His Mob was gone. They'd taken it. Rats! Still, hard luck for them if they tried to mess with it – unless the correct code was put in when it was activated, a small phial of acid would be released to burn out everything of interest inside. If a person had it in their hand when that happened – ouch!

Fortunately, they hadn't emptied the other things from his pockets.

He crouched, laying out the three ordinary-looking objects on the floor. A small circular box of dental floss. A retractable ballpoint pen. A pack of chewing gum.

He'd practised with these Project 17 devices so often, he could almost have assembled them with his eyes closed. Unwrap the gum and wad it up into a ball. Push it into the lock on the door. Unwind the floss and embed one end in the gum. Get at least one metre away from the gum before unscrewing the pen and winding the floss around the exposed inner cylinder. Screw the pen up tightly again. Click the end quickly three times to arm the thing. Turn your back. Press down on the top of the pen. Count to four, then release.

Whump!

There was a small, contained detonation and a flash of light. Zak stood up and walked to the door. The area around the lock had melted, giving off a few wisps of smoke. Zak pushed at the door. It swung open.

He stepped out into Bree Van Hausen's office. It was empty and the doors were closed. He looked around with a trained eye. He spotted an ornament – a small bronze statue of a diving woman. He picked it up and went over to the doors, pushing the statue through the handles. If anyone came back, that would slow them down for a while at least.

He went to the desk and sat down. He drew Bug's memory stick from its hidden pocket and slid it into a USB port.

The screen lit up with the familiar Worldwide Synergy logo of the planet Earth showing the Americas on one side and Europe and Africa on the other. A sub-page appeared and letters and numbers began to scroll down faster than Zak's eyes could follow.

The time on the computer read 21:13. He glanced out of the window. The sky was dark but the Los Angeles skyline was ablaze with lit-up tower blocks, stretching away into the distance.

He was aware of an odd noise. Not especially loud,

but constant and heavy. He couldn't quite make it out. Something to do with the building work, he guessed. Byron Venn had said it was going on around the clock.

There was a soft *ping* from the computer. Bug's little gizmo had done its job. A password box had opened. The password was filled in as a row of dots. Zak clicked on enter.

The screen changed.

His eyes widened. The image of planet Earth was still there, but now it was encircled by another more sinister image. A fire-red snake with its tail in its mouth, entirely surrounding the Earth. And filling the space where the Atlantic Ocean would have been were the fiery letters **WS.**

Worldwide Synergy?

Zak watched as the flamed danced.

WS

World Serpent?

He moved the curser onto the letters and clicked the mouse.

A new page opened.

World Serpent Manifesto. Our Aims and Purposes.

Terror is a means to an end.

World Serpent will use whatever means necessary to fulfil its great destiny. As captains in my army, you each have your own orders and your own missions to accomplish. But understand that each of you is but a single cog in a great global machine.

The great warlords of antiquity performed marvellous deeds. Alexander the Great created one of the largest empires of the ancient world, Attila the Hun devastated the Roman Empire, Genghis Khan subdued the Asian continent. Ivan the Terrible controlled an empire of one and a half million square miles. But we will do more. We will bring down every government in the world. We will create mayhem and strife. We will create warfare and destruction on a scale that the old warlords never dreamed possible.

**And from the anarchy and the
lawlessness and the desperation that
will engulf the world, we will rise
and we will take power and there will
be no one to stop us.**

Our mission has only just begun.

Reaperman.

Zak sat and stared at the page, hardly able to take in
what he was reading. It sounded crazy. It sounded
impossible. And yet . . .

He looked again at the name at the foot of the page.

Reaperman.

The shadowy figure who had ordered the deaths of his
parents. The international terrorist whom the secret
services of the entire world had been trying to locate.
The man that Zak's own brother had gone into deep
cover to track down.

The manifesto made one thing clear. Reaperman
was Raging Moon's boss. And she was just *one* of his
captains. How many more were there? Dozens of them

scattered across the world? Each of them plotting death and destruction. It was too much to take in.

So much confusion and horror filled Zak's brain that he could hardly think straight.

This was huge. Reaperman wanted to control the world – and he was prepared to commit any atrocity to make that happen.

But it could never work. No one was powerful enough to do that.

Were they . . . ?

Colonel Hunter and Assistant Director Reed had known about the organization called World Serpent, or at the very least they knew the name and something about the threat it represented. So why refuse to tell him and Wildcat the truth? Why keep it hidden?

It made no sense.

Zak pressed keys in a specific order, as he'd been trained to do. The memory stick began to download files.

His head snapped around at the sound of someone rattling the door handles.

Only about fifteen per cent of the stuff had been downloaded so far.

The rattling grew louder. He heard shouting. Something heavy began to crash against the far side of the doors. Raging Moon's people wanted in.

Zak stared around the room. There was only one way out – through those doors. And it sounded as if there were three or four guys out there.

He'd need to take them by surprise.

The memory stick had only downloaded eighteen per cent.

It was no good. He had to go for it, before the doors were beaten open. He grabbed the stick and shoved it into his pocket. He just hoped that eighteen per cent would be enough to give them a lead on Raging Moon's plans.

He ran to the doors. They were being given a good pounding. The statue was rattling and he could see that the handles wouldn't hold much longer.

He moved about three metres back, breathing deeply and slowly, getting ready. He dropped into a sprint-start position, one leg drawn up under him, the other trailing, his body balanced on fingertips and toes, his eyes focused on the place where the two doors met.

With a final boom, the doors flew open.

There were four men in the doorway, Byron Venn and three heavy-set men in suits who looked like a bad version of nightclub bouncers. Zak made for Byron – he was the smallest of them. He still had the gun, but Zak didn't give him the chance to use it. He leaped high, one knee striking Byron in the face, his other foot coming down on the man's shoulder, hands on his head. Using Byron as a springboard, he flew through the air and landed at a run. The glass rooms were deserted now, but the lights were still blazing.

He sped along the corridor. The banks of lifts appeared. One door was open. No. Not a good idea. One quick call from Byron Venn and there could be a whole gang of security guards waiting for him at ground level.

He made a sharp left turn and headed off into unknown territory. He heard shouting and running feet behind him. Ignore them. Focus on the way ahead. Find some stairs. Stairs were good. When he was in the zone, he could ricochet down entire flights of stairs like a rubber ball. They'd never catch him.

Except he couldn't find any stairs. And although the men chasing him weren't getting any closer, he could hear them yelling instructions – which meant they were in touch with others. That could be bad. They knew this place. Zak didn't. They could get other people to head him off.

He crashed through double doors. Stairs! At last. He went for it, legs tucked under him, arms spread for balance, sailing down to the lower landing, bouncing off the floor onto the wall and zigzagging down the following flight.

He sped down ten floors before he glimpsed men running up a lower flight towards him. He barrelled through the doors on the next landing and pelted along a hallway. More glass-walled rooms, more desks with computers.

He found another stairway and managed to descend another two flights before some dark-suited men appeared below him.

Rats.

He dived along another corridor. This one was different from the others. Unfinished. Hung with polythene sheets. No glass walls, no carpets. Why was that? Byron Venn had said they were building another tower, not renovating this one.

Then he got it. He shoved his way through a huge hanging plastic sheet and found himself staring out of a large hole in the wall of the tower. A temporary walkway jutted out, made of scaffold poles and long slabs of metal. It met with more scaffolding surrounding the part-constructed framework of the new tower.

Zak guessed this was going to be some kind of bridge between the two towers. He glanced back. He could hear running feet. But there was a louder noise, too – the noise he'd heard only faintly from Raging Moon's office. A deep, gurgling, splashing noise that reverberated all around him. He still couldn't quite make out what it was.

He looked down, and by the glare of floodlights, he finally saw what was making the noise.

Three floors below, at ground level, a huge machine was pouring liquid concrete into a massive metal-lined hole. The concrete was coming out of a long hose, bubbling and blooping as it spread. He couldn't see any workmen. He thought they must be inside the huge industrial-scale cement mixer, or maybe the whole thing was on automatic?

What had Byron Venn told him? They were sinking the foundations of the new tower. Yes, that made sense. A tower block would need a pretty solid base – and it looked as though this one was going to be built on a layer of several thousand tonnes of concrete.

He heard the snapping of the plastic sheets behind him. He saw the dark shapes of the pursuing men. He sprinted out onto the walkway, and then jumped down to a horizontal scaffolding pole. He landed well, spreading his arms to keep his balance before flexing his knees and jumping down again to the next pole. He paused, steadying himself with one hand on a side pole.

He stared over the network of scaffolding. At the far

side, about forty metres away, he could see some kind of hoist mechanism with pulleys and ropes. If he could get to it, he'd be able to use it to make his way down to the ground in style.

Excellent!

He picked his way across the poles to where planks had been laid across the scaffold. The walkway was narrow and unsteady, but he had wicked free-running skills. He'd make it, no problem.

He glanced behind him. He could see some of the men who had been chasing him standing on the metal walkway between the towers. He grinned. They were milling around, looking baffled.

Then he saw one of them shouting and pointing.

There was the crack of gunfire. A bullet whined as it struck off the scaffold pole right next to his head.

A bit too quick with the grinning, Zak!

He raced along the planking, arms out, fingers stretched, his eyes locked on the way ahead. In the zone. He heard the searing whine of a second bullet. Too soon to feel safe. Too soon to think he'd beaten them.

He heard the smash of broken glass. The bullet must have gone through a window. He looked up again. The network of planks and poles meant he couldn't see them. It also meant that, for the moment at least, they couldn't see him. He was almost at the hoist – but maybe there was a quicker way down? He paused, teetering on the edge of the walkway, staring into the great gurgling vat of wet concrete.

There was a metal collar around the top of the huge circular hole. If he judged it just right he could drop from here and land safely on the collar. Then it was just a couple of metres to the ground. A sprint across the building site, a leap over the fence and away.

Yes. Worth the risk.

He looked down again. The drop was no more than four metres. He could do that. Easy.

He took a deep breath, steadying himself. Then he jumped.

But he hadn't realized that the metal collar sloped towards the hole – and he hadn't reckoned on it being so slippery. He lost his balance, slithering down, his arms wheeling. His foot caught on the edge, his hands snatching at nothing as he fell into the hole.

It took the first of the men a couple of minutes to make their way to ground level. Two of them climbed the steel ladder to the collar of the metal-lined foundation hole.

A man in orange overalls and a hard hat climbed

down from the operating cab of the huge cement mixer.

"What happened?" he gasped. "I thought I saw something."

"You saw nothing," said one of the men. "Get back where you came from. Just do your job."

The workman hesitated for a moment, staring at the two men in fear and dismay. Then he turned and walked rapidly away. He knew what kind of men these were. He wasn't going to risk confronting them. Anyway, they were right – maybe he had only thought he'd seen something. Maybe it was nothing.

The two men climbed onto the metal collar, edging carefully forwards.

Four metres below them, they saw a dark shape in the liquid concrete. The back of a leather jacket with a golden eagle on it. The jacket the boy had been wearing. Even as they looked, the dark shape of the jacket sank into the concrete. There were a few bubbles. Then nothing.

One of the men took out his mobile phone and pressed speed dial.

"He's dead, ma'am. No doubt about it." A pause. "Yes, I understand that, but we didn't kill him, ma'am. He fell. Am I sure he's dead? Uh . . . pretty sure. He fell into the wet concrete. He got sucked under before we could do anything."

The man pocketed his mobile again. He nodded to his companion and the two of them climbed down and headed back up to the fifteenth floor.

The zippy little Brit brat was history.

And if things went to plan, in twelve hours, another one and a half million residents of the city of Los Angeles would be joining him.

Wildcat brought the Harley Davidson to a skidding halt on the far side of the road from Sable Tower. The evening had closed in over Los Angeles and the sky was pitch black, but down here, in the canyon streets, with lit-up tower blocks all around, it was almost as bright as day.

She kicked off again, nosing through the slow-moving traffic, steering the bike off the road and in a long curve around the building. There was some pretty heavy construction work going on, she could see that. A whole area alongside the tower block was fenced off, and she could see scaffolding and floodlights and hear industrial noises.

She parked the bike behind some portacabins then walked around to the plaza. She strode up to the main doors and peered in. The foyer was deserted except for a reception desk. She pressed the entryphone button.

"Yes?" a disembodied voice answered.

"Jet Speed Couriers," she said into the grille. "I'm here to pick up a package from Bree Van Hausen of Worldwide Synergy."

There was a click and the door glided open.

She was walking over to the desk when a buzzer sounded. The man at reception picked up a phone. He listened for a few seconds then slammed his hand down on something that Wildcat couldn't see.

A door opened and half a dozen men in dark suits appeared. One of them was listening to instructions through an earpiece. He gestured to the stairs and the men chased after him.

Wildcat watched them from behind her tinted visor. She knew trained guards when she saw them. Something was going on. Something to do with Zak, maybe?

She came up to the desk. "What's up?" she asked.

"Sorry, the building's been locked down," said the man. "I can't let you into the elevator for the time being."

"Oh, great," said Wildcat. "I'm already running late. How long is this going to take?"

"Hard to say," said the man with a shrug.

"What kind of emergency is it?" she asked.

"I couldn't say.'

"Can I use your phone to call my boss?" Wildcat asked, moving around the big reception desk. "You can explain why I'll be missing my deadline."

"Knock yourself out," said the man, handing her the receiver.

Wildcat smiled under the visor. *Love that American expression!*

She sprang forwards and headbutted the man. He slithered off the chair with a low groan.

"Sorry," she murmured. "No time to explain."

She turned and ran for the stairs. If she was right about the nature of the emergency, then she needed to tag along and hope she could help Quicksilver out of whatever mess he'd walked into.

She kept back as the men made their way up the staircase, always within listening distance, pressing against the walls so they wouldn't see her.

"He's coming down the south stairway," the leading man announced. New info on his earpiece, Cat guessed. "Aaron, Jeff, Parker – you carry on up here, I'll take the others along to the south stair. Watch yourselves, guys, the kid is fast."

Wildcat smiled grimly to herself. *The kid is fast.* No prizes for guessing who they were talking about.

She hung back as the men split up, then she followed

the leader and his little gang off the stairway and along some corridors.

They came to the south stairway. Wildcat paused by the swing doors.

"There he is! Go get him!"

There was the rattle of shoes on the stairs – heading upwards. Wildcat ran into the stairwell. Through the tall windows she could see scaffolding. Below her, a massive sunken tank was being filled with liquid concrete.

She was about to fling herself up the stairs when she saw a movement on the scaffolding above.

It was Zak. He was picking his way across the scaffold poles like a high-wire artist in a circus. As she watched, he bounded from pole to pole till he came to a series of wooden walkways. He was on a level only a few metres above her. She heard a shot ring out. Zak flinched then ran.

Wildcat pulled off her helmet. Gripping it in both hands, she swung it at the window. There was a shattering peal of glass. She used the helmet to knock out the remaining shards, and climbed onto the frame. She balanced herself, took a breath, then jumped for the scaffolding.

She was one level below Zak. He needed to know she was there. He needed to know he wasn't alone. But before she had the chance to call out, she saw him jump.

He landed on the metal collar that surrounded the sunken foundation hole. She saw him slip. Slither. Fall.

She made a desperate leap down onto the sloping metal walkway. She landed heavily, on hands and knees, her whole body jarred by the impact. She scrabbled to the inner edge and stared down. Quicksilver was about a metre below her, clinging by one hand to a chunk of jagged metal.

"Silver! Grab my hand!" She leaned out as far as she dared, stretching her hand down, her fingers straining. He looked up and she saw fear on his face. He reached for her hand. Their fingers nearly touched. But not quite.

She risked leaning down further. She felt the pack shift on her back. Something bumped against the flap. Silver stretched for her hand again, and this time their fingers locked around one another's wrists.

Cat felt something slide out of the backpack. She saw a thin silvery object plunge down past Silver's body.

The laptop!

It knifed into the wet concrete two metres below Silver's feet. The thick grey concrete closed over it in a matter of seconds.

Straining to her utmost, Wildcat pulled Silver up the wall of the tank. He got a foot over the edge and rolled onto the metal walkway.

Cat didn't have time to think of the implications of losing the laptop. She needed to act fast.

"Give me your jacket," she gasped. "Now!"

Silver slipped his jacket off. She pulled the backpack off her shoulders and wrapped his jacket around it. She flung it into the concrete.

It lay on the surface for a moment, then began to sink, the golden eagle design clearly visible.

With any luck, the men chasing Silver would think he was still wearing it.

She grabbed his hand and they raced for the far side of the vat. It was only a two-metre leap down to the ground. They didn't speak. They jumped, both of them landing lightly. Cat beckoned and Zak followed her. They vaulted the perimeter fence of the construction site.

Three minutes later, they were on the Harley Davidson, speeding through downtown Los Angeles.

Rescue mission accomplished.

CHAPTER **TWELVE**

Wildcat drove beyond the outskirts of the city. She turned the bike into a steep side road and headed for the hills. She finally brought them to a stop alongside a wooded slope. They dismounted and she walked the motorbike in under the trees.

They'd been going so fast that Zak hadn't been given the chance to say much more than 'thanks'. Cat threw herself to the ground, her back against a tree. She wiped her arm across her face. "It's hot in these leathers," she said, unzipping the jacket.

"I'm glad you turned up when you did," said Zak,

sitting at her side. "But how come you were there at all?"

"I'll tell you my story, then you tell me yours," said Cat. "It started when I got a vid-link call from Bug . . ."

After they had brought each other up to speed, Wildcat insisted they try to catch a couple of hours sleep.

"We'll be fit for nothing if we stay up all night," she explained. "And we need to lie low for a little while. They might think you're dead, but they'll certainly be looking for me. The gate guard at the Parnassus Mansion will tell them I stole a bike. Once they know that, it's not going to take them long to put two and two together and figure out that I was the person in the leathers at Sable House. Let them hunt for me up and down the city. We can rest up. We'll need it. One way or another, I think we have a pretty heavy day ahead of us tomorrow."

They slept under the tree for two, maybe three, hours. When Zak woke, Wildcat was already sitting with her back against the tree, her legs drawn up, her arms wrapped around her knees, staring out at the rough outlines of the Santa Monica mountains against the dark blue skyline. He had the feeling she was deep in thought. He waited a while before speaking.

"I really liked that leather jacket," he said at last. He wasn't seriously that concerned about the loss of the jacket – it was just something he could make sense of – but the rest felt too big to take in. It had all come rushing back when he had woken up. Reaperman was behind World Serpent – and World Serpent wanted to take over the world. Who can cope with something as insane as that?

"On the positive side, they think you're dead," Wildcat replied. "Which means they won't be looking for you, just me."

"Crazy Woman said they weren't planning on killing me any more, anyway," Zak reminded her. "They wanted to take me off somewhere and mess about with my insides to see how I work."

"Even better then," said Wildcat. She glanced around at him. "I wish we hadn't lost the laptop. I can't believe that happened."

"They took my Mob as well," Zak said. "I hope one of them tried to use it. A hand full of acid would serve them right."

"I still have mine," said Wildcat. "But I'm not going to activate it unless I have no choice. Control was concerned enough about it not being totally secure before we found out Crazy Woman knows about Project 17."

It had taken them a while to decide what to call Aurore Marat. In the end they had decided "Crazy Woman" would do just fine. It suited her.

"How does she know?" asked Zak.

"And *how much* does she know," added Cat. "My guess is the information originally came from Colonel Pearce."

Yes. That made sense. Colonel Pearce must have passed a whole lot of top-secret information to her Italian contact before Zak and Gabriel shut her down. The *Ouroboros* had been in Venice at the time. From Pearce to Padrone, from Padrone to the *Ouroboros*, and from the *Ouroboros* to Raging Moon.

"But that doesn't explain how they know about *this* mission," said Zak. "Unless there's another mole."

Cat shook her head. "I don't think so," she said. "Work it out for yourself. Mr Dean gets suspicious of you, and he tells Raging Moon. Then what happens?"

Zak took up the tale. "Raging Moon checks up on me," he said. "World Serpent must have a database of information about Project 17 and all the other secret departments of MI5. I know Control changed all the pass-codes and stuff like that, but the basic information about people like you and me can't be changed. So, they run a check on my face and find a match. Agent Quicksilver of Project 17."

"Got it in one," said Cat. She looked at him thoughtfully. "We're up against a really huge organization, Silver."

"Tell me about it," said Zak, blowing his cheeks out.

There were a few moments of pensive silence between them. They had a lot to think about. A lot to take in.

"You get that we're entirely on our own now, don't you?" Wildcat said at last. "I'm not going to use my Mob – and we shouldn't try to contact Fortress or Assistant Director Reed on an open line." She gave a grimace of frustration. "And we're still no closer to knowing what they have planned."

"Crazy Woman said that in twelve hours a lot of people were going to wish they had *hydro*-something-or-other," said Zak. "It was meant to be a clue."

"Hydrophobia?"

"Yes, that was it," said Zak. "What is it?"

"Rabies," said Cat. "It's called hydrophobia because one of the symptoms is that people panic if they're offered water." She shook her head. "No one would ever wish they had rabies. Unless it's treated instantly, it's nearly always fatal."

"Perhaps she was messing with me," said Zak.

"No, wait," said Cat, her eyes narrowing. "There's something else about water. Something I overheard on the *Ouroboros*."

"You mean the toast the guy made? *Here's to sweet Los Angeles water*?" said Zak, remembering what she had told him.

"With our special additive," Wildcat finished. "Our *very own* special additive."

Zak stared at her. "There's a location shoot at a water pumping station today," he said. "At the Oakleaf Canyon Water Pumping Station."

Cat looked up at the gradually lightening sky. "It's almost dawn." She sprang up and ran for the motorbike. "We have to get over there," she called back. "They're going to poison the water!"

Zak leaped up and raced after her. He could remember the tone in Crazy Woman's voice quite vividly. *In twelve hours about one and a half million people in Los Angeles are going to wish they had hydrophobia. It's going to be a big day tomorrow. A day no one is ever going to forget.*

Wildcat was already astride the motorbike. She kick-started it. The engine roared as she twisted the throttle. Zak leaped on behind her.

"Do you even know the way to the Oakleaf Canyon Water Pumping Station?" he asked as she steered the bike out from under the trees.

"I do," said Cat. "I've been studying maps of this whole area ever since we got here."

"You know which roads will take us there quickest?"

She looked at him over her shoulder. There was an odd, fierce, determined light in her eyes.

"Who said anything about roads, Silver?" she said.

She gunned the engine. With a roar, the Harley Davidson went skimming across the road and over a grassy hump onto a steep hillside shrouded in trees.

"Hold on tight," she called, leaning in low over the handlebars. "This could get wild!"

THE SECOND LOS ANGELES AQUEDUCT. OAKLEAF CANYON WATER PUMPING STATION.

The Second Los Angeles Aqueduct was constructed in the 1960s to increase the supply of fresh water to the city of Los Angeles. Drawing its water from the Haiwee Reservoir in the Eastern Sierra Nevada Mountains, it runs underground for the most part, using 3.7 metre wide steel pipes. It is 220 kilometres long and delivers water to over one and a half million residents of Los Angeles. That's over forty per cent of the city's population.

The Oakleaf Canyon Water Pumping Station is the final point at which the water is quality-checked before it enters the city's residential and industrial system; the final time it is analysed for purity before coming out of people's taps.

If, say, a terrorist with no concern for human life wanted to put something deadly in the water supply, this would be the perfect place to do it.

But the pumping station is surrounded by a high wire fence, patrolled by guards and watched constantly by CCTV cameras whose images are relayed directly to the local police station. If anyone tried to make an unauthorized entry, the police would be there within minutes.

The only way to get close enough to the pumping station to do any damage would be to infiltrate the buildings under the cover of some legitimate activity.

Something like a location shoot for a movie, for instance.

Operation Hydra had been planned meticulously and to the last detail. It only took Bree Van Hausen and her six dark-suited thugs a few minutes to lock down the pumping station once the gates had been opened for the trucks and trailers and other vehicles of the *Adrenaline Rush* location shoot. Two of her men stormed the main security room, taking the guards by surprise and quickly introducing a virus into the CCTV system so that the cameras locked into a continuous loop – a loop that showed everything was fine.

Two others, armed with automatic machine guns, subdued the perimeter guards and locked them up. The final pair fired their weapons into the air to make sure no one was going to play hero, then corralled the entire movie crew into an open space between their parked vehicles. They were secured with plastic ties around their wrists and ankles and forced to sit on the ground while the two men stood watchfully over them.

Only one man was left free.

Bree Van Hausen – Raging Moon – stood in the control room of the pumping station, staring towards the main gate through the wide window and checking her watch every few minutes.

Elton Dean sat in a chair close by, pale, sweating, on the verge of panicking. A pain was nagging in his chest. It had been there for several hours. "What happens next?" he asked.

"You'll see soon enough," she said coldly.

"When are you going to send your ransom demands?" Elton Dean asked.

"You're an idiot," Raging Moon said dismissively, not even looking around at him.

The sweat poured down Elton Dean's face. The chest pain really was intense. "What if they don't comply with your demands?" he asked. "You won't really set the bomb off, will you?"

She gave him a contemptuous look. "There is no bomb, Elton," she said. "There never was a bomb."

He stared at her. "But you said . . ."

Bree Van Hausen had approached him several months ago. Her proposition had been very straightforward. "*I need your help, Elton. I work for some very dangerous people. If you don't help me, they will kill all your family and friends, one by one. They will burn your mansion to the ground. They will destroy Parnassus Studios. Then, when you've lost everything you ever held dear, they'll come for you, and you'll die slow and hard. Will you help me? I'll give you two days to make your mind up.*"

He had been shocked and alarmed, but it had taken an unexplained fire at the studios the following night to convince him she meant business. After the fire, she had come to him again.

"*The people I work for are, I guess you'd say, career criminals. But things are getting too hot for them in California. The police are breathing down their necks.*

They feel it's time to do one last job and then get the heck out of Dodge, know what I mean?"

Frightened now, he'd asked what she needed from him.

"It's simple. You're mounting a major movie shoot. At the climax of the movie, the bad guys hole up in a pumping station on the Los Angeles Aqueduct, and threaten to blow the place sky-high unless their ransom demands are met. Well, we want to do it for real. You have the contacts in the city to get approval to shoot in the Oakleaf Canyon Water Pumping Station. Once we're in, we're going to set the bomb, then we're going to get in touch with the big guys in City Hall, and we're going to demand a five-million-dollar ransom. Otherwise we blow the pumping station up and disrupt the water supply for almost half of Los Angeles."

Elton Dean thought she was crazy – or the people she worked for were. But the fire at the studios had convinced him of their ruthlessness, and when he'd recovered from the initial shock and tried to back off, the death of Chet Blake and the threat to his family had proved to him that he had no way out.

It was bad. It was very bad. But the city would pay up. The criminals would get their money and they'd vanish. And no one would ever know he had played a part in the crime. And . . . and it might even be a real publicity boost for the movie. Who wouldn't want to go and see a movie where the big finish had happened for real?

So, what did she mean . . . there never was a bomb?

"I lied to you about the bomb, Elton," she said. "I tell lies sometimes. I'm sorry, but that's the kind of girl I am."

His eyes widened. "This is a *bluff*?" he gasped. "You're going to try and extort five million dollars and there's no bomb?"

"I lied about the five-million-dollar ransom as well," said Raging Moon. "We have something else planned."

He stood up. "I demand to know what this is really all about!" he shouted as the pain surged under his ribcage.

She turned on him like a snake, her arm swinging, her fingernails ripping bloody trails down his cheek. He fell back into the chair, holding his hand to his face, renewed fear in his eyes.

"I'm waiting for a tank truck to arrive," Raging Moon told him, icy calm again. She turned back to the window as though she didn't think he was worth the trouble watching. "The tank truck will be carrying several thousand gallons of liquid cyanide. We're going to introduce the cyanide into the water system."

Elton Dean was so shocked he could hardly form words. "Why . . . would . . . you do . . . that . . . ?" he gasped. "Thousands of people . . . could be killed . . . why . . . ?"

A smile crept up one side of Raging Moon's face. "A lesson in terror," she said. She glanced at him. "You know the problem with most terrorist organizations, Elton?" she said sweetly. "They think too small. The people I work with, they think big. They think globally." She made a sweeping gesture. "This is just the start," she said. "This is going to seem like a pinprick in relation to what World Serpent has planned." Her eyes gleamed. "We're going to bring down every government in the world, Elton. There's going to be chaos and death and destruction on a scale no one has ever dreamed of. And then, when every country on Earth is in turmoil, we're going to move in. We have resources you can't imagine, Elton. We're going to take over the entire planet."

"You're insane." Elton Dean's face was twisted with horror.

She turned to him, her face oddly blank. "That's a really dull thing to say, Elton," she replied coolly. "I expected something better from you." Her mobile phone rang. She held it to her ear. "Yes?"

A wide red smile broke across her face. She ran to the window. "Yes. I see it. Excellent. Open the gates, Byron. Let them come on in. It's almost show time."

On the long winding road that led up to the main gates of the pumping station, a tanker was slowly driving. A tanker loaded with almost eleven thousand litres of liquid cyanide.

Zak and Wildcat lay on the crest of a hill overlooking the Oakleaf Canyon Water Pumping Station. Zak was wearing his Project 17 issue sunglasses with the zoom on maximum.

"Okay," he began. "I see two armed men at the main gates – one of them is that Byron guy who bashed me. The movie trucks are in a parking space near our side of the perimeter fence. The crew is in an open area between the trucks and trailers. They're all sitting down. I think they're tied up. Two more men are watching them – both armed. I can't see Crazy Woman. I guess she's in the buildings somewhere."

"Do you see any vehicles that you don't recognize from the movie convoy?" asked Wildcat. "A different truck or something?"

Zak scanned the gathered trucks and trailers. "No," he said. "What am I supposed to be looking for?"

"If they plan on putting something nasty in the water supply, it would have to be kept in some kind of mobile container. And there would need to be a whole lot of it."

"Got you," said Zak. "No, there's nothing. Oh! Wait." His

eye was taken by a movement on the road that wound up through the hills towards the pumping station. He touched the side of the sunglasses to try and get a bit more zoom out of them. "Uh oh."

"What have you seen?"

"A tanker. Making its way up the road that leads to the gates," Zak said. "Crazy Woman has a really weird sense of humour."

"In what way?" asked Cat.

"I've just seen what's written on the side of the tanker," Zak replied. "It says 'Sweet Los Angeles Water'."

"Oh, very cute!" said Wildcat. "That has to be the poison." She frowned. "Okay, this is where we need to come up with a plan of attack. Do you have any bright ideas to get us started?"

Zak stared at her. There were at least four armed men down there. There was a tanker loaded with poison arriving at the gates. There was a Crazy Woman in charge. And there was just the two of them to stop it happening.

"Yes," he said after a few moments. "Yes, I do."

CHAPTER **THIRTEEN**

"What the heck . . . ?" Byron Venn ran forwards and stared through the gates. He had only closed them a couple of minutes ago, after letting the tanker through. Something strange was happening out there.

A motorbike came bouncing down the hillside towards the road, still on its wheels, but without a rider. Smoke was pouring from its petrol tank. The motorbike hit the road, slewed around and crashed onto its side, skidding across the tarmac and coming to a halt a few metres away.

Byron glanced up the hill. Had someone been doing some off-road motocross riding? Had they fallen off? If that was the case, why couldn't he see anyone?

His thoughts were shattered by a fierce explosion. A ball of fire erupted from the motorbike as its fuel tank ignited. Byron backed away from the sudden flash of heat. Burning petrol spilled from the ruptured tank, spreading out over the road. Fire snaked towards the gates.

Byron grabbed his companion by the shoulder. "Get something to put this out," he shouted over the roar of the flames. "Go! Now!"

The man stumbled away.

The leaping flames had reached the gates now. Standing back and shielding his eyes, Byron got on his mobile to Bree Van Hausen.

Something screwy was going on.

90 SECONDS EARLIER.

Zak ignited the rag sticking out of the petrol tank and pushed the motorbike down the hill. He dropped to the ground and crawled rapidly out of sight. He wasn't certain his plan was going to work the way he had imagined it. The bike might just topple over on the hillside and that would be it.

From cover, he peered down the hill. Yes! The bike was still upright. Good plan! It bounced down onto the road and fell on its side, its momentum sending it sliding towards the gates.

Perfect!

He belly-crawled over the crest of the hill, then he got to his feet, and ran. Now it was Wildcat's turn.

Go for it, Cat! Ruin Crazy Woman's day!

Wildcat was crouching in a small hollow on the hillside behind the pumping station. It was the last piece of cover before the outer fence. She couldn't see the road from here. She was listening intently. Waiting for the right moment.

She heard the motorbike explode.

Go!

She sprang from cover and raced down the hillside. She didn't have Silver's speed, but with any luck, everyone's attention would have been drawn to the gates by the noise. She flung herself to the ground, up against the fence.

There had been a small leather roll strapped to the side of the bike. A few tools for an emergency. One of the tools was a pair of wire cutters. Wildcat got busy cutting through the bottom of the fence. It was hard work, but she used both hands on the cutters and soon there was a small gap through which she was able to slither.

The nearest of the movie trailers was only two metres away. She made a dash for it, slid underneath and crawled to the far side. She could see the movie people now. They had been tied by their wrists and ankles, and were sitting in a frightened huddle. Hiding behind the rear wheel of the trailer, Wildcat scanned the familiar faces, looking for someone in particular.

The armed men were staring towards the gates, as were most of the movie people. Grayson Clarke was there, as well as Scott Blaine and the other actors. One face was missing, Cat noted. Elton Dean.

But Cat was looking for a different face. A grey-haired, bearded face. The guy who had explained to her how the pyro devices were going to work on the boat when they'd been out in Paradise Cove.

There!

Cat crawled under the trailer, dived for another truck and dragged herself close to where Mitch Miller sat with his back to a wheel.

"Mitch?" she projected the whisper. No response. "*Mitch!*" Slightly louder this time.

Mitch looked around and an expression of amazement came over his face.

"Olivia? How did you get here? We were told you and

your brother quit."

"I don't have time to explain right now," hissed Cat. "Listen, I need your help."

"They've got us pretty much locked down, Olivia," said Mitch, turning away from the two armed men, his voice a low whisper. "I don't know what these people want, but they're armed, and they mean business." A few people close by looked to see what was going on, but they were smart enough not to give the game away.

Wildcat reached out from under the truck and used the wire cutters to snip through the ties holding Mitch's writs together. "Don't move yet," Cat warned, putting the cutters in his hand. "But start cutting people loose as soon as you get the chance."

"They're watching us all the time, Olivia," said Mitch.

"I'm going to give them something else to look at," Cat whispered. "Listen, Mitch. I need to set up a diversion. And I need your help to do it."

"What do you need?"

"I need you to tell me how to set off all the explosives you keep in your special effects truck," said Cat. She'd already spotted the truck. It was a big black Ford with chrome trim and the word PYRONAUTS on the sides. The truck had been parked a little distance away from the others. They always did that, in case of accidents. If Cat blew it up, there shouldn't be any casualties. She hoped.

"You got it," said Mitch. "Now, listen really carefully, Olivia. Mess this up and you're history, right? This is dangerous stuff."

Wildcat flattened herself against the back of the black truck. So far so good. She released the two catches on the shutter and pushed it up – slowly, carefully. The shutter rattled softly. Shhh! She lifted it just high enough to slip in through the gap. She lay still for a few moments, letting her eyes get used to the gloom.

Mitch's instructions were going round in her head. She stood up and began to hunt through the truck for the things she'd need. A plastic box labelled 'black powder'. A can of gasoline. A detonator and a roll of wire. The smallest of the portable control boxes.

Working as quickly as she could, Cat assembled a small pyro device in the middle of the truck. It was hot, and sweat dripped into her eyes as she fed the cable towards the back of the truck. She had no idea how long this was taking. Had she been in the truck for two minutes? Five? Ten? Her Mob was in her pocket, but she didn't dare turn it on. If World Serpent had been given access to Project 17's greatest secrets, how could she be sure they wouldn't home in on her the moment her Mob went live?

But if she took too long, Crazy Woman would win. Raging Moon could be feeding the poison into the water system right now.

Wildcat slipped out of the truck and ran for the cover of the nearest other vehicle, carefully feeding the cable out as she went. She sat behind the car and attached the wires to the terminals on the control box. She paused, breathing deeply, waiting for her hands to stop shaking. This was fiddly work. She couldn't do it if she was in a panic.

She stayed there until the beating of the blood through her temples slowed a little. Wiping the sweat from her eyes, she screwed down the terminals.

One and a half million people were in danger.

One and a half million!

She flipped the red switch to make the control box 'hot'. She closed her eyes, praying that she'd done everything right.

"Fire in the hold," she murmured as she pressed the button. "Please let there be fire in the hold!"

Zak made his way stealthily around to the far side of the

pumping station. He hunkered down behind a chunk of rock about five metres from the fence. He had no more idea how quickly time was passing than Wildcat did. He just had to sit there and sweat it out – and hope that Cat succeeded in her part of the plan.

His crazy plan.

Time crawled by.

Come on, Cat – come on!

The explosion sent a plume of fiery black smoke roaring into the sky. The noise was still ringing in his ears as he jumped up and ran down towards the fence. He could see flames leaping away beyond the main buildings of the pumping station. Wildcat had done it. He only hoped she'd got clear before the pyro truck had gone up.

He jumped for the fence. Climbing quickly, he rolled over the top and leaped down to the ground. He sprinted for the building, in the zone in an instant, covering the open space in seconds. Not even out of breath. He stopped under one of the windows. That had been the easy part of the plan.

He slid along the wall, looking for an entrance. He found a side door at the top of a short flight of concrete steps. The door was locked but there was a narrow frosted-glass window right above it. The metal-framed window was propped open. Zak eyed the slender slot thoughtfully.

Easy.

Probably . . .

He crouched, judging the distance and the power he would need, then he sprang upwards. He gave himself an extra boost with one foot on the door handle. His hands grasped the lower edge of the window frame. He dipped his head and curled his spine, his shoulder blades scraping on the open window as he slid through. He felt the metal edge graze his calves and heels as he dived. He used his momentum to generate the power to flip himself over and land feet first, knees flexed for the impact.

Perfect!

He was in.

He ran light-footed along a plain corridor lined with doors. The rooms beyond were offices and store cupboards. Not what he was looking for. He came to a door with a glass panel.

The door was at the top of a long flight of metal stairs that led down to a huge work area filled with steel piping and complex machinery. This had to be the heart of the pumping station. Zak could hear the noise of the machinery, and he could feel the floor vibrating under him as thousands of litres of water were pumped through those massive pipes.

A tall shutter was open at the back of the pumping room and the tanker with 'Sweet Los Angeles Water' printed on it had been driven in.

A heavy-duty metal-ribbed hose snaked along the ground from the back of the tanker. A man was busy with a large spanner, unscrewing a valve cover on one of the huge pipes.

Raging Moon was there, dressed all in red as usual. She looked angry. She was shouting. "Ignore it, you morons! Help Ross with the hose."

Two men with machine guns were standing at the open shutter, staring out. Zak guessed they were looking at the flames from Wildcat's explosion.

"It could be the Feds!" one of them shouted.

"What if it is?" Raging Moon snarled. "They can't get in here in time to stop us."

Zak slipped through the door. No one was looking up. He padded softly along a high gantry that ran around the upper wall. A metal ladder was clamped to the wall, leading to ground level. He glanced down again, his heart racing. Not from the effort, but from a moment of doubt and anxiety. Could he pull this off?

He gripped the rail, trying to calm himself.

The two armed men had come back. They had picked up the end of the hose and were standing close to the man called Ross. He was lifting the cover off the valve.

"Screw the hose on," said Raging Moon. "Ross. Get back to the cab. Start the pump on my word."

Ross ran for the front of the tanker.

This was it. Zak had to move quickly. He climbed onto the ladder and went down hand over hand at top speed. Ross was climbing into the cab of the tanker as Zak hit the ground. He was now hidden from Raging Moon and the other two.

He raced for the tanker.

"Go! Go! Go!" he heard Raging Moon shout.

Zak flung himself desperately at the tanker, ripping the door open and hurling himself into the cab. He saw Ross flip a switch. A look of startled alarm swept over the man's face as Zak's hand came chopping down at the side of his neck.

Zak had practised the Krav Maga chop a thousand times in training, but he'd never used it in the field before. He knew how it was meant to work – strike the carotid sinus just right and it interrupts the blood flow to the brain and renders your opponent temporarily unconscious.

Zak felt elated and relieved as Ross slumped silently forwards.

It had worked.

Zak reached past him, one hand opening the driver's door, the other pushing him so that he toppled out of the cab. He threw himself into the driver's seat. Learning to drive any kind of vehicle was standard training for all Project 17 agents. He wrenched the gear lever and slammed his foot down on the accelerator pedal. The tanker lurched forwards. He flipped the pump switch into the off position as the tanker jerked out under the shutter.

Zak leaned out of the open window to see what was going on behind. Yes! The hose had broken away from the back of the tanker and was writhing on the ground. Nothing was coming out of it! No liquid! No poison! He'd shut off the pump in time.

Raging Moon ran towards the tanker. "Stop!" she shouted. "Shift into reverse, you idiot!" Then she saw Zak's face at the tanker's window. Anger and disbelief twisted her expression. "No!" she screamed. "No!"

But even as she stood staring at Zak, a brief gush of liquid sprayed out from the back of the tanker, catching her full in the face. She staggered backwards, slipped and fell into the deadly pool of liquid cyanide.

Wrestling with the wheel, Zak drove the tanker out of the building. The vehicle was cumbersome and unwieldy, and it took all of Zak's strength to keep it under control as he brought it to a skidding halt. A noise above his head made him peer upwards through the windscreen. A grin spread across his face.

The cavalry had arrived.

The size of the explosion took Cat by surprise. The heat seared her face as she watched the special effects truck go up in flames. A couple of metres closer and she'd have lost her eyebrows. Still, Silver's plan needed a diversion – and now he had one. A big one.

Cat ran, skirting the other movie trucks. The two armed guards were staring at the ball of fire that was rising over the movie vehicles. Cat sprinted behind them. She threw herself sideways, crashing into the first man's legs and tipping him over backwards. She was up again in an instant. The second man turned, aiming his machine gun. But Cat's shoulder drove into his stomach before he could shoot. The man doubled up and collapsed on the ground.

Reeling a little from the impact, Cat grabbed the man's gun, running over to the other man and kicking his gun out of reach.

"Stay where you are!" she shouted, aiming the machine gun at the two sprawling men.

She heard voices behind her. Mitch had managed to release some of the movie people, and they came swarming forwards.

"Olivia, you did it!" called Mitch Miller. "Attagirl! That was outstanding. Give me the gun, I'll take it from here."

"You do that," said Cat, handing over the machine gun. "Don't let them move." She ran for the buildings. Had Quicksilver fulfilled his part of the plan?

She raced around the side in time to see the tanker driving out through a shuttered entrance. Silver was at the wheel.

Now the noise of the tanker's motor was drowned out by a new sound. A sound that came from the air, a sound that was growing rapidly louder.

She stared up.

Helicopters.

Black FBI helicopters. Three of them, swooping low over the pumping station, stirring up the dust as they came in to land.

The helicopters settled on the ground. The sides opened and armed FBI agents jumped out.

Zak leaned out of the tanker's cab. "It's okay!" he yelled to Wildcat. "The plan worked!"

He saw Assistant Director Reed jump down from the lead helicopter.

"How did you know where we were?" Zak called to her in amazement, leaping out of the tanker and running to join Wildcat.

"Bug told us how to track the GPS signal from Wildcat's Mob," said Assistant Director Reed. "We just followed your trail."

Of course! He should have remembered – the GPS app in the Mobs was active even when the phones were switched off.

"None of the poison got into the water supply, I'm pretty certain of that," Zak told her breathlessly. "But Crazy Woman was right in the line of fire when the hose broke loose – she got a face-full of it."

Assistant Director Reed put her hands on her hips, looking from one to the other of them. "So," she said. "Do you two agents want to fill me in on exactly what's been going on here?"

CHAPTER **FOURTEEN**

FBI FIELD OFFICE, WILSHIRE BOULEVARD, LOS ANGELES.

Zak and Wildcat sat facing Assistant Director Reed across a wide desk. AD Reed had a mission file open in front of her. She was reading from it.

"The terrorist codenamed Raging Moon died from ingestion of a concentrated cyanide solution at zero-nine-hundred hours at the Oakwood Canyon Water Pumping Station." Her eyes rose briefly to Zak. Wildcat was looking at him too. Did they think he'd feel sorry for Raging Moon?

No way.

"I didn't kill her on purpose," he said. "But I'm not sorry she's dead. As far as I'm concerned, she deserved it for what she was going to do."

"Fair enough," Cat said with a smile. "I couldn't have put it better myself."

AD Reed nodded and carried on reading aloud. "Six other terrorists were apprehended without injury," she said. "They are currently in a special facility at Edwards Air Force Base, pending full interrogation."

Zak grinned. Cat had taken down the first two gunmen, and as soon as the Feds had arrived in their three big black helicopters, the other four had surrendered their weapons without firing a shot. He could still remember the cheering and applause from the liberated movie people. He and Cat had been paraded around on their shoulders. It wasn't often Project 17 agents received that kind of appreciation at the end of a mission.

"Elton Dean was found dead in the main control room of the pumping station," Assistant Director Reed continued. "We are still awaiting a forensic report to ascertain the cause of his death, but early indications are he had a massive heart attack."

"The stress would have done that," said Cat. "He must have freaked when he found out what Crazy Woman was actually planning to do."

Zak thought she was probably right. Elton Dean had been a total idiot, but no way would he have agreed to kill a million and a half people. Brutal as it sounded, he was probably better off dead.

Assistant Director Reed nodded, but continued to read. "Production on the film *Adrenaline Rush* has been halted; the New York backers have pulled out and it is unlikely now that the film will be finished."

Zak felt quite disappointed about that, though with Elton Dean dead and with the businessmen in New York backing off because of all the bad publicity, there was no way the movie could carry on.

"An FBI team raided the *Ouroboros* in the Mendocino Holiday Harbour," AD Reed continued. "Ten crew members were apprehended, but it is not thought that any of them were part of the team that organized the attempted terrorist attack on the Oakleaf Canyon Water Pumping Station. The yacht has been impounded, pending further investigations." She turned the page. "The attempt to pollute the water supply of Los Angeles with cyanide was thwarted in no small part by the actions of agents Quicksilver and Wildcat of British Intelligence. The FBI would like to extend their gratitude to Colonel Hunter and the whole of Project 17 for their cooperation in bringing this mission to its successful conclusion."

Assistant Director Reed looked up again. "Are you guys happy with that?"

"Very," said Cat.

"Absolutely," added Zak. He paused for a moment. "But . . ."

A faint smile appeared on AD Reed's face. "I was waiting for the 'but'," she said. "Peter told me there was always a 'but' with you."

Zak had to admit there was some truth in that, but this was a particularly important "but".

"You haven't mentioned World Serpent at all in the report," he said. "But we know Crazy Wo— I mean, Raging Moon, uh, Bree Van— well, you *know* – she was working for Reaperman, and Reaperman is the boss of World Serpent. I told you what I found on her computer."

AD Reed nodded. "Unfortunately, by the time we got to her computer, its hard drive had been fried, and the files you managed to download all concerned Worldwide Synergy. There was no mention of anything else."

"But I *saw* it – I saw the picture of the snake around the Earth, and I told you about that manifesto thing," said Zak. "Why isn't that in the report?"

AD Reed closed the file and leaned back in her chair. "I don't have the authority to answer those questions, Quicksilver," she said quietly. "Perhaps there's someone else you'd like to ask?" She shuffled some other files on her desk and drew out two air tickets. "We've booked you seats on a flight out of LAX this evening," she said. "You're going home. Honour is due, guys. Honour is due."

FORTRESS, LONDON.

"I've read Assistant Director Reed's mission report," said Colonel Hunter. "You both did good work over there." He looked from Wildcat to Zak. "As I would have expected."

They had been whisked from Heathrow Airport to Fortress and brought straight into Colonel Hunter's office without even the chance to dump their bags or get a change of clothes.

"I have also spoken with Assistant Director Reed," the Colonel continued. "She tells me there was a question asked that she was unable to answer."

"Silver asked about World Serpent," said Wildcat. "There was no mention of it in the FBI report. I'm sorry, but I don't get it. Why the silence?"

Colonel Hunter looked at them for a few moments,

as though weighing up his options. "Very well," he said, getting up. "Come with me."

He led them to the main briefing room.

"I'll be explaining this in greater detail to all the other agents in due course," he said, closing the door and locking it. "But I think you deserve to hear about it immediately."

He gestured for Zak and Cat to sit facing the giant plasma screen that filled one wall. He picked up a remote. A map of the world appeared on the screen. The map was dotted with red circles – they were everywhere, sometimes scattered thinly, sometimes appearing in clusters.

"This map shows where terrorist attacks or attempted terrorist attacks have taken place over the past three years," the Colonel told them. "As you will see, every continent has been affected – Europe, Africa, Asia, North and South America, Australia." He clicked the remote and a smaller number of dots began to pulse with red light. "An international alliance of intelligence organizations has been monitoring these incidents, including the FBI, MI5, the Russian FSB, the IAS in Japan, and the intelligence gathering departments of many other countries. As head of Project 17, I have been involved in this for some time now. The incidents highlighted here are all believed to have come from a single coordinated terrorist organization."

"World Serpent," said Zak, his eyes moving from one pulsing red dot to another, through Europe, across Asia and all the way to America. "You're talking about World Serpent."

"We have agents in deep cover across the globe, gathering information and passing it on to a central command station." The Colonel paused for a moment before continuing. "I am not at liberty to tell you where that command station is situated. Recently, the name World Serpent has been coming up with greater and greater frequency. The World Serpent organization was certainly involved in your mission in Montevisto. Padrone, the secret agent in Venice, was also part of the organization."

"And Reaperman is the boss," said Zak. "The guy who had my parents killed."

"We've known that someone codenamed Reaperman was behind the organization for some time," said Colonel Hunter. "I asked you not to discuss the name World Serpent because it was vitally important that Reaperman should not discover how close we are coming to unmasking him. We do not know to what extent his organization has infiltrated international intelligence services. We could not afford for our agents in deep cover to be tracked down and neutralized."

Colonel Hunter clicked the remote again and the image of the *Ouroboros* appeared on a sub-page. "Thanks to the work you two agents did in Los Angeles, we've achieved a major breakthrough."

Zak leaned forwards, his stomach tightening into a knot, his mind whirling.

What was Colonel Hunter about to reveal to them?

"Quicksilver, you've been asking about the agent codenamed Slingshot for some months now," said the Colonel. "I'm finally in a position where I can reveal that he has been located here." The world map zoomed in, centring on the Mediterranean Sea, closing in on Greece. "Slingshot has been based in Greece for the past three years. Among other potential leads, he has been investigating a very secretive and suspicious man names Achilles Rhea." A new sub-screen appeared, showing a slideshow of surveillance pictures of a particular man. Zak guessed he was in his mid-fifties, with a rugged, deeply tanned face, a grey moustache and a wild mane of grey hair.

"Achilles Rhea is a multi-millionaire businessman with interests throughout Europe," the Colonel told them. "His various businesses are also thought to be a cover for wide-ranging criminal activities." The map zoomed again to show a small cluster of islands. "These islands lie in the southern Ionian Sea off the west coast of Greece," said the Colonel. "The largest of the islands is called Panos. That is where Achilles Rhea has his main home. Slingshot had never been able to find a convincing link between Rhea and any known terrorist groups." He turned to Zak and Cat. "You two have given us the evidence we needed."

Zak was thinking fast. What evidence? Then something clicked. Something Bug had told him.

"Does he own a TV company in Greece?" he asked.

"He does," said the Colonel. "Carry on, Quicksilver. What's the link?"

"His company owned the *Ouroboros*," Zak said eagerly. "The same company that was bought up by Worldwide Synergy."

"Clever boy," murmured Wildcat with a grin.

"Correct," said Colonel Hunter. "Except that we've done some further investigation and it turns out that it was Achilles Rhea who bought Worldwide Synergy – not the other way around."

"Achilles Rhea is Reaperman?" asked Wildcat.

"The evidence we have so far makes him our prime suspect," said the Colonel. "But we daren't make any false moves. We have to be certain before we try to take him down. I've been in contact with the international alliance, and I've been asked to set up a mission designed to get final proof. Project 17 is considered the perfect department to do this, and in a few days a select group of Project 17 agents will be travelling to the island of Panos."

"Have you decided who?" Zak asked urgently. His long lost brother Jason – aka Slingshot – was in Greece. He had to be part of the group being sent there. He *had* to be.

"I have," said Colonel Hunter. "I'm sending a team of five agents. Switchblade, Moonbeam, Jackhammer, Wildcat . . ." There was an agonizing pause. ". . . and Quicksilver."

Zak's heart beat hard against his ribs. There was a strange hollow where his stomach should be. He felt light-headed.

The plasma screen went blank. Colonel Hunter walked to the door, unlocked it and threw it open. "There will be a full briefing for all the agents involved in Operation Icarus tomorrow at zero-six-hundred. Meanwhile, the two of you look as though you need a shower and some sleep. I want you both fully rested. In two days' time I'm sending you to Panos to bring down Reaperman." His eyes glittered as he looked from one to the other. "This is the most important mission you have ever been on," he said. "The fate of the world will be in your hands."

Zak walked to his room in a daze. The fate of the world! Wow! But it wasn't the thought of destroying World Serpent that was filling his head right then. It was the idea that he would finally get to meet his only living relative — that he'd finally come face-to-face with his long-lost brother Jason.

He crashed onto his bed, his eyes wide open, his mind racing.

He could not wait for Operation Icarus to begin.

Turn the page for a sneak preview of Zak Archer's next mission:

End Game

CHAPTER **ONE**

THE ATLAS MOUNTAINS. MOROCCO.
LATITUDE: 32.361403°
LONGITUDE: -1.977539°

Zak Archer lay flat on a high ridge overlooking the ruined old Foreign Legion fort of Jebel Lekst. The sun was just rising over the parched landscape of rock and scrub, throwing sharp-edged shadows over the broken peaks and deep canyons of the Atlas Mountains.

Zak glanced to his left. Switchblade was hunkered down about twenty metres away. Further off, where the ridge curved towards the fort, he could make out Moonbeam's red hair between two jagged fingers of rock. To the right, Jackhammer and Wildcat were waiting for the word.

Switch was group leader on this operation. The five of them had travelled all night to get here, bumping along a narrow earth track in their Range Rover, headlights off to lower the risk of them being spotted from the air or from distant peaks. Moonbeam had been at the wheel. She was trained to drive anything with wheels or wings.

At fourteen years old, Zak was the youngest of the group; Wildcat was fifteen, the others were all sixteen. But they were all skilled agents in the specialist department of British Intelligence called Project 17. And they had a vital mission to perform in this inhospitable landscape. The fate of the world might well rest on them getting it right.

Zak turned back to the fort. It was brown, with a rectangular outer wall surrounding a group of low, square buildings. It almost looked like an elaborate sandcastle that had been left to crumble away in the sun. He put the Hotscope binoculars to his eyes again and immediately all the colours and shapes morphed into a weird pattern of blues and pale greens.

He was scoping for orange or red.

The blue-green end of the colour spectrum meant cold, lifeless. Orange-red showed heat and life. They'd had to be here early for this. Once the sun began to beat down on the valley, everything would turn furnace-red and there would be no chance of spotting a body moving about.

Zak roved his Hotscope over the buildings.

Nothing.

Now what? Would Switch order them to advance and hope for the best? What if the German agent codenamed Isabel wasn't there any more? What if their intel was wrong and she'd never been there?

He let out a sharp breath. A small splinter of red had appeared from behind one of the buildings – just for an instant. Then it had vanished again.

"Target acquired," Zak murmured, knowing the microphone of the Imp in his ear would relay his words to all his fellow agents. The Imp was an extraordinary new piece of kit, no bigger than an earplug, it contained a microphone and receiver that gave pinpoint reception up to five hundred metres.

"Where?" Switch's voice came in his ear.

"Front right building," said Zak, his heart starting to beat faster, his body tingling and ready for action.

"Someone poked their head out from behind then disappeared again."

"Certain?" asked Switch.

"You bet," said Zak.

"Okay, guys," came Switch's voice again. "We're moving in. Keep to cover. Moon and Hammer, I want you round the back. Cat and I will take the sides. Silver, in through the front, okay?"

"Got it," said Zak. His codename was Quicksilver. The name suited his particular abilities, as he imagined Isabel was about to find out.

One by one the heads of the others drew back. Zak shuffled forwards on elbows and knees, peering down the steep drop, plotting a way down. A kind of rough-edged fissure ran sideways down the cliff-face, like a scar. The perfect cover.

He scrambled over the brink and slithered into the narrow groove. He made his way down the cliff, then, darting from boulder to boulder, he sped towards the fort's half-ruined gateway. The gates were long gone and one of the towers had fallen in on itself.

He caught a glimpse of Switch racing across the sand to his left.

He paused for a moment in the cool shadow of the gateway tower. There was about ten metres of open ground between him and the entrance to the building where he'd seen the red image.

Stealth wouldn't help him now; he needed speed.

Taking a single deep breath he broke cover and ran for the dark oblong of the doorway. He was in the zone in an instant – in that amazing place where his mind and his body locked together and he could outrun the wind.

He was through the doorway in moments, moving smoothly and effortlessly, feet kicking up the dust, arms moving like pistons at his sides.

The light was dim and grainy in the building as he ran from room to room.

He found her crouching in a back room, dressed in desert camouflage fatigues, a peaked cap low over her eyes, a backpack on her shoulders. He had a brief impression of large black eyes and shoulder-length black hair. But the thing that stopped him for a moment was how young she looked.

Colonel Hunter had told them Isabel was in her teens – but it had never occurred to Zak that she might be no more than his age. Apart from twelve-year old Bug, the computer genius back in Fortress, Zak was the youngest agent in Project 17. Did this mean there were other organizations like Project 17 all over the world?

He only had a split second to register the thought

before Isabel's arm shot out and Zak was forced to duck to avoid a missile flying at his head. It was a can of baked beans, one of several food cans stacked in the corner of the room. Provisions for hiding out here in the middle of nowhere.

"Hey!" Zak cried, narrowly avoiding the can. "We're not ..." He got no further. She launched herself at him. He saw an expression of concentrated fury and determination on her face, then her shoulder hit his midriff and he was thrown onto his back, winded and gasping in pain.

He was still sprawling on the ground as she sprang up and raced off. He clambered to his feet. He glimpsed her silhouette in the glassless window for a moment, then she was gone.

Wow! She was fast!

But he knew he was faster.

Gritting his teeth, Zak sprinted after her, clearing the window frame in one smooth leap. She was running for a gap in the back wall of the fort. He focused, slipping easily back into the zone.

He saw Jackhammer appear at the edge of the broken section of wall. Hammer was a big guy – built like a rugby forward. He'd stop her, no problem.

Zak slowed as Hammer stepped into Isabel's path

and spread his arms. Isabel jinked to the side as he snatched for her. Almost without breaking stride, she high-kicked him in the chest and rocketed past, leaving him staggering and gasping.

She was good.

Zak sped up again as she sprinted away from the fort.

"Nice try, Hammer," he said. "I'm on it."

Zak smiled to himself. Hammer was very competitive, he'd hate it that he'd failed where Zak was about to succeed.

Isabel was sprinting up the far slope of the valley now. Impressive. But Zak was on her heels before she'd gone even a quarter of the way.

Careful. She's a tricky one. He didn't fancy taking another hit from her. As he ran, he slipped the Taz out of his pocket. It looked like a slender black rubber torch, but it had a powerful battery and pincer-like electrodes at the business end. Touched against exposed skin it gave an electronic kick that could take down a grown man. The effect was only temporary, but it got the job done.

Isabel glanced over her shoulder. Her face registered surprise that he was so close.

Yeah, sorry about that. The super-speed thing gets them every time.

Zak was about to tag her with the Taz when she put on a spurt of speed that made him feel as if he was standing still.

What was *that*?

Stones and dust rained on him as she ran up the hillside. He only let himself be stunned for a moment. Then he went after her at top speed.

He concentrated hard, digging deeper into the zone. But still she was ahead of him. What was going on?

She vanished over the hilltop.

Zak came flying up to the ridge. The hill fell away into a steep ravine. From there he could see Isabel, already halfway down the far side, leaping and jumping from rock to rock like a mountain goat with a sugar rush. Zak had never seen anything like it.

Taking a deep breath he plunged after her. He had one thing clear in his mind: Isabel was no ordinary agent. She was easily as fast as him, and she had all his free-running skills.

Colonel Hunter hadn't warned them about this.

If Zak didn't pull something out of the bag pretty quickly, she'd get away.

And that would be a disaster. Not just for Project 17, but potentially for everyone on the planet.

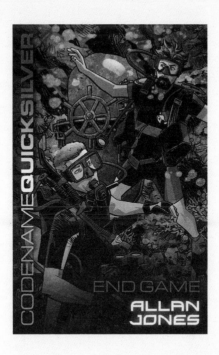

Zak Archer is a spy, working undercover for Project 17 –
a government agency so secret, it officially doesn't exist.

An international terrorist organisation has developed
a device which can wipe out entire cities in seconds.
Project 17's job: to stop it being used, whatever the cost.

Failure means global destruction, death and chaos.
This is Zak's most dangerous mission yet, and he'll need
everything he's ever learned if he's going to survive it.

978 1 4440 0550 9

£5.99

the orion star

Sign up for **the orion star**
newsletter to get inside information
about your favourite children's authors
as well as exclusive competitions and
early reading copy giveaways.

www.orionbooks.co.uk/newsletters

Follow   on

Orion
Children's Books